OHMHOLE

OHMHOLE
TYLER HAYDEN

BookThug · 2011

Cover illustration by Fraser Wright
Copy edited by Ruth Zuchter

The production of this book was made possible through the generous assistance of the Ontario Arts Council and the Canada Council for the Arts.

ONTARIO ARTS COUNCIL
CONSEIL DES ARTS DE L'ONTARIO

Canada Council   Conseil des Arts
for the Arts   du Canada

LIBRARY AND ARCHIVES CANADA CATALOGUING IN PUBLICATION

Hayden, Tyler, 1985–
   Ohmhole/ Tyler Hayden.

ISBN 978-1-897388-95-2

   I. Title.

PS8615.A838O56 2011   C813.6   C2011-904776-4

PRINTED IN CANADA

Elliott

The Spade, new weeks old, hones on nothing new. The darkened room, a lone lightbulb sways, left of the bed, right-to-left, left-to-right and back and stops. The light cuts an oval on the floor, wood, roughed. Outside the oval, the floor might be wood too. From this angle it's difficult to tell anything.

They brought me here, shaved me, scrubbed me, and told me I'm dying. I have seen little evidence of the latter. They being them to put it dimly. They gave me clothes: a bed, white sheets, blue cotton blankets thinning in the right places. They have not given me clothes. The blanket is my clothes. I roll myself into jointed warmth. The blanket catches the excess shit and piss perfectly. All shit and piss is excess. The cleanings happen efficiently and unknowingly. This has not changed and will never. The cleanings are signaled by the smell of bleach. A lot can be learned from the smell of bleach. Nothing can be learned from the smell of bleach. All the clothes fit perfectly because I rolled them myself. At least they got something right. They got nothing right.

I don't think I'm dying. I've seen little to no evidence of this. I'm both sick and healthy. I'm both angry and calm. I'm both ugly and attractive. I'm being treated and have always been. It's out of disgust that they treat me. No. It's out of desire they treat me. No. The two are confused because they are confusion. I'm dumb. I'm unsure who will hurt in this situation. Their treatment eats at me: pills, powders, silence, unknown cleanings. The Spade: the box migrates clear around the room. Copper metal arcs my skull ion burnt. The blue light digs in then out of my forehead, cozy with a copper buzz that bites on night, afternoon and day. I'm getting ahead of myself, more about the Spade will come if there's time. There's no time.

Actually, the buzz sounds more like a hum.

Unstitched electrons whirl 360 degrees in and out of my skull on loop.

Blood is defective: details leak in awkwardly often.

My voice is a voice of others because that's all there is in our skulls.

My illness is unknown: I know everything about it.

My illness is a cure.

My illness is me.

The lightbulb pulls itself up into the black of the ceiling. The oval of light dissipates. The morning light creeps through the window now to the right. My mind pockets, never been better. The window diffuses itself.

Karms

He is my doctor, apparently. Even though he has never said so directly: he just refers to himself as "Karms." He is tall, bald, with eyes, a nose, lips, but mostly forehead. He speaks and will speak indirectly. He comes into my room and stands over my feet observing them. "A lot can be learned from people's feet," he says. "That's stupid," I say. He then nods in agreement with me. "Are you enjoying your stay at St. Nowhere?" he says. "That name is fake," I say. "All names are fake," he says. I then nod in agreement with him. He speaks to me indirectly through his eyes, which look down and seem to mouth the words he is thinking, his lips rarely move. That is a lie. His lips move but they twitch like a cat in heat. That is a lie. By heat, I mean fire. I mean his lips twitch like a cat being burnt alive. That is a lie too, but it is a lie that most people will prefer. He looks at me and tells me things. The vagueness is intentional. We deeply mistrust each other. We like it that way because we are forced to. "Write stories," he says. "Why?" I say. "People like to read stories about people dying," he says. "Why?" I say. "I don't know," he says. "What kind?" I say. "Of stories or people," he says. "Stories," I say. He doesn't say anything. "What do I write with?" I say. "With the Spade," he says. He points to the box between my knees. "With that piece of shit, you're stupid, seriously, with what?" I say. "Just write," he says. "Write with what?" I say. He nods. I say, "my shit, my finger and the bedsheet," and he says, "yes," and I say, "with my shit, my finger and the floor," and he says, "yes," and I say, "my shit, my finger and the Spade," and he says, "yes" and I say, "my shit, my finger and the walls," and he says, "yes, if your legs permit," and I say, "my legs will permit," and I say "my shit, fingers and the pillows," and he says, "yes," and "I say my shit, my fingers and the mattress," and he says, "yes," and I say, "my shit, my fingers and the door," and he says, "yes, if I can get that far," and I say, "I will," and I say, "my spit, my finger and the bedsheet," and he says, "yes," and I say, "my spit, my fingers and the floor," and he nods and I say, "my spit, my fingers and the Spade," and he nods and he goes to look out of the window and I say, "my spit, my finger and the pillows," and he nods and I say "my spit my fingers and the mattress," and he nods and I say, "my spit, my finger and the door," and he says, "the same as before as with the shit." He appears open to possibilities. "What are the stories going to be used for?" I say. "To wound boredom," he says. "If I have time," I say. "You will," he says. "Probably," I say. "Why do people write stories about death?" I say. "To introduce a possibility into the universe to ensure that it won't happen to them, their loved ones, or anyone else again or other. Life, the universe, whatever, tends towards chaos or unpredictability or uncliché. Anything written becomes cliché and therefore not likely to happen. And if it does happen it will be a time when the cliché is forgotten and returned to the realm of unpredictability, not to the fault of the original text, but to our faulty and frayed collective memory," he says. "That is the stupidest thing, shut your fucking mouth," I say. He goes quiet. "What about fear?" I say. He says, "that too."

Zip-lock

Every morning or afternoon or evening, the pillman comes. The flush of envelopes under the door. Gold foiled envelopes: ART written on them, black-labeled.

Saint gets the envelopes first. He walks to the front door. The backs of his pants skim against the tiles. He bends down, shaggy hair falling. A terry cloth towel covers the window. He hunches down and collects. The keys looped around his belt-loop chime. The keys have no function and are just for aesthetics. He carefully stacks the envelopes on top of each other, staggered for no reason, walks to the kitchen table, and drops them. He goes to the cupboard and takes down two glasses, goes to the fridge and takes out a plastic zip-lock bag filled with pink and blue pills. He walks back to the table and puts the glasses and bag down.

He opens the bumpy envelopes and fishes out the pills. In the envelopes there are numerous possibilities of colors, none more infrequent than others: zero blue, six pink: one blue, five pink: two blue, four pink: three blue, three pink: four blue, two pink: five blue, one pink: six blue, zero pink. Today, there are six pinks for no reason. He puts two in one glass, one in the other. He drops the remaining three into the bag.

He goes back to the front door. Kicks the piles of shoes. Under the

9

piles of sweaty leather, he finds Preeti's soiled slip-ons. He picks them up and holds them up to verify. He organizes all the shoes against the wall.

He walks back into the kitchen and takes down another glass. He fishes two pinks from the bag and drops them into the third glass.

He goes back to the stained couch and takes a smoke from a black-labeled pack on the coffee table. He tries to strike three matches from a book but none take. He rubs his stubble.

Still 1.01

I stand in my room in the Motel against the door backlit by two panes
of mercury. Shadows rope better at night: Saturday best. My naked
chest replays a photograph of my father sharpening a knife on a black
stone half oval, then back over. My father's picture reloads. His stubble cakes up. I don't know what I'm thinking: I'm thinking where I
am. Every 2 ribs accumulate 1 finger.

Motel

St. Nowhere stinks white. The doctor stinks: the air stinks: the silence stinks: the boredom stinks: the food tastes like cum. I'm going to edge out into memory because that's a dump I can handle because it's in my skull: localized boredom.

The ceiling and the floor collapse into static nausea at even rates.

The Motel is where we live. Saint runs it. Runs isn't right. Saint has a real name but it doesn't suit him so we never use it. Saint doesn't suit him either: it's a stupid name. Every name fits him like an anal fissure. He was here before any of us came. He's tall, skinny, shaggy hair, young with broken teeth, wrinkles presumably from meth, dull green eyes. His pants never fit right. The Motel isn't much of a motel: another stupid name too. It's an old housing complex up from the river, half-burnt collapsed. The wiring works sometimes. I don't know how. The front door to the building is boarded up. Boarding up doors only draws more attention to them than anything. The only entrance is in the back, up a faded blue wood staircase. Below the staircase lies a small patch of dirt and plastic that doubles as a toilet when the water isn't working. Saint says he used to grow ground vegetables, mostly carrots, potatoes. I don't believe him. He's hardly sober. He hasn't planted for as long as I've been here. I don't know how long I've been here. Now he grows ripped plastic, rust, and broken needles. At the top of the stairs, there are two doors, only one of them can be reached, the right door is the front door to Saint's. The left has no balcony anymore, fell a little while ago, can't remember when. We tried nailing a two-by-four from the stair railing to the wall but the wall crumbled worse. We had some plastic lattice there for a bit, but it fell too. Nothing currently fits there. Both the doors, no, the door to the right is boarded fake, left is real boarded. On the right, the planks and two-by-fours are only nailed to the door and not the frame. The door opens, no problem. Through the door, a dirty walkway scuffs glass plastic baggies, a bathroom on the left, a bedroom on the right, kitchen after. I say kitchen out of habit, it's not really a kitchen, but kitchen will do. In the kitchen, there's a door to the left that opens to the front staircase. The staircase leads down to the boarded front door of the building, broken furniture piles at the bottom black. This left door is the only way to get into our place. It's called the left room right now. Because I have to give it a name. We don't have names for things like this so I have to make them up now. We only give names to things that last as long as we do. I'm not creative. This section has nothing in it. There will be more interesting things later but not now. Wait it out.

Left is where I stay or Preeti stays when she comes by. I'm here more than she is. She's usually out fucking and cutting. She comes when she feels like it. The left is nothing. Through the door, there's directly a kitchen. It's not really a kitchen, I've said this before. To the left, there's a stove, the elements spiral rusty, thick with melted plastic like dried semen. A sink for when the water works. Taps for when the water works. When the water doesn't work and we're out of bottles, we use the rain or snow barrels and boil with the kettle or a perk coil, if there's power, if not we have a fire, if we can't get a fire going, we're fucked for the night or however, fire, that's how the other half of the building went. I don't know. I just thought of it. Next to the sink are plates, piles of plates or stacks of plastic baggies stuffed burned with cigarette butts. Just the butts. Try to smoke them down to the butts.

Or pick every last nail of tobacco and reroll. Waste is as waste does. The counter is dusty. The cupboards are bare. Occasionally there are dishes or plastic bottles. Nothing frequent enough. After the counter is a hallway. To the left is a room with a mattress. The door, the back door, boarded. This door goes to nowhere as there is no balcony on the other side. This is a refresher. Left of the door is another room empty. This room is not empty. It is the bathroom. My favorite room. I'm not sorry about the mistake. All rooms are the same in memory. A small rectangle: mirror, counters, basin, toilet, tub. I'm the only one who cleans it. I like cleaning it. I take an old shirt and rip it, try to get as many rags as possible, usually I get eight including the sleeves. Sleeves work the best because you just slide your hands in with the thumb out like a glove. I use the powdered bleach. Depends on whatever is given on Monday or Wednesday maybe Tuesday. The powder is good because there's more time before it mixes with the water and starts to eat at your hands during the scrubbing. Rubber gloves are hard to get. Saint used the last ones to cook the vials, haven't seen them since. The bleach cracks the knuckles first, then works its way to the skin between them, leaves the hands purple for days. I start with the toilet first. Work the bowl, then work my way up then back down to the floor. Cold piss and cigarette butts stain rings in the toilet bowl. We only flush for solids, so piss, cig butts, half lice, hair sit until then. Our bowels are so backed up with nothing, we flush only once or twice a day. I sprinkle some on the rim and in the water, until the water looks milky lime. I flush, then scrub the yellow rings, shit, blood etc., as the water slides down the sides. After the bowl is clean I open the window and toss the rag out, aim to the left, flutters a story, lands on the balcony on the ground a trash pile now. Grab another rag, sprinkle water on the underside of the upright seat, rub over with bleach and water. Toss, flip the seat down, sprinkle, rub, toss. Work the underside of the lid, sprinkle, rub, toss. Flip the lid down, sprinkle, rub, rub the metal lever, toss. Around the hinge, sprinkle, rub, rinse, but no toss. I use the same rag for the floor around the toilet, sprinkle, rub and toss. Then the mirror, sprinkle a bit on, wet, rub, toss, don't care if there's streaks. Work the counter, sprinkle, rub. After the toilet, the basin I care for the most. The basin is metal, painted, or whatever white. A large rust circle circles the drain. This is my favorite spot in the left room. I've looked at this spot for hours. White metal eaten away by rust that won't stop. The rust won't stop until it has eaten through it all. But right now the circle is perfect. No. Not a perfect circle, there are no perfect circles, there might be perfect circles but I'm unaware of them. Then there's the drain hole: black stinks violent. The whole basin looks like an eye. Bloodshotted circle: rust circle: black circle. I care for this eye more than my own. I sprinkle the bleach and rub the outer edge of the rust the hardest to help it spread. After I'm finished with the eye, I toss the rag. I glance at the bathtub. I never clean the bathtub. Piss on the thing. To the right of the bathroom, there's the kitchen, this is repeated, a table, where we eat, if we get the powders. The fridge sometimes works. We rarely put anything inside it. Saint keeps the pills. I don't know why we have one: aesthetics maybe.

Through an archway is the family room. It smells of shit and/or red sulphur. There are three mattresses: one where Preeti fucks and two safeties for when we're too cracked to get back to our room. Her fuck mattress is by the left wall: blood stains in the center of the mattress: 70s flowers: blood layers on blood layers dries into another flower. She bleeds heavily monthly. I rip piles of t-shirts for her too and put them beside the mattress. Others sleep on her mattress too, but I don't know who they are. The blanket she uses crumpled kicked to the bottom with blood on it, naturally. The other mattress by the right wall under the window is mine, has less to no blood. A broken speaker and mixer stands under the window propping up a pot of broken records. I pile my clothes there orderly but farther away. To the right of the archway is our room: another mattress to the right in front of a window with a view of cables and a transformer. The best part of the room is the door and its two hinges. Nothing else really matters to me. This is the end of left.

Deus Ex Welfare

Every week on Monday or Wednesday maybe Tuesday, I forget, on the street corner, they toss from their rust trucks 4 bundles labeled BUNDLES with black marker, for whoever gets to it first:

The outside contents vary:

Towel: cotton or not, small to medium, undyed, may have BUNDLES written on it, black-labeled

Shirt: cotton or not, small-to-medium, used or new, various colors, may have BUNDLES written on it, black labeled.

The inside contents vary:

Razors: 2, disposable, plastic handles, dull to sharp, new or used.

Sodium Bicarbonate: white powder, medium plastic baggie, black-labeled, knotted or not.

Sodium Hypochlorite: white powder, medium plastic baggie, black-labeled, knotted or not.

Socks: cotton or not, medium to large, new.

Azithromycin or Doxycycline or Erythromycin: 1 blister pack, black-labeled, expiry date blacked out.

Medical tape: plastic, maybe 2.2m, new.

Gauze: cotton or not, small to medium, new.

Soap: a bar, unscented, tiny bird stamped on.

Protein: white powder, medium plastic baggie, black-labeled, knotted or not.

Vitamins: white powder, medium plastic baggie, black-labeled, knotted or not.

Minerals: white powder, medium plastic baggie, black-labeled, knotted or not.

Carbohydrates: white powder, medium plastic baggie, black-labeled, knotted or not.

Cigarettes: 2 25's, white slip, filtered, black-label.

Isopropyl 99: plastic bottle, 500ml, new or used, black-labeled, expiry date blacked out.

Water: 3 plastic bottles, 500ml, new or used, black-labeled, expiry date blacked out.

Teeth

My mother sits on the corner of the bed, cut by the hallway's light-bulb, slits through the door. The quilt, a patchwork of denim and orange yarn. She, a vertical itch in the squares, rubs my ankle bone. Her tin ring roughed and wire thin on her thumb, dull in light. Her hands reddened from dishwater, darker than her arms. Slight smell of bleach. Her short brown hair triangles a widow's peak, points to her lips, splinter dry.

Nights are broken waisted.

"Night," she says.

She shuts the door to my room. The worn handle shifts horizontal metal. The room turns incomplete darkness. My animal nightlight glows by the door, slouching black ears, white face, black eyes, belly a bump of sun. I say animal generically because most animals are all dead now. The Coke crates, coat hangers, cement blocks, all angles of dark.

My abandonment issues reside with LIFE not with my mother to clarify.

Fuck Freud: psychoanalysis is piss poor astrology.

I have always swallowed my teeth. For as long as I can remember. They rattle against my cheeks. Ball down my tongue. If you suck on them they chalk apart tasting of exhaust. If you bite them they sugar then nothing, tasting of blood. I have always swallowed my teeth. Low into my chest.

Tonight, I wait a couple minutes before I check for the tooth fairy. You never know with her. If she's late or early. She comes every night. In through the radiator and up the curtain. Or in with the sliver of light under the door, a short fat crawl. I feel through the pillow with the back of my skull for her.

My hand slides under the pillow. I feel her hair: rat warm yarn. Soft stubby arms. Studded denim overalls. I pull her out from under my pillow. In the glow of the nightlight, she looks cracked. A pocket stitched onto the denim of her little overalls with tiny rivets. Inside the pocket, I finger out a little tooth. A smooth tooth, polished and slightly chilled, pink or blue.

I'm in the kitchen on an unrelated morning:

"This, this is a tooth," – my mother says, holding a pink tooth in her hand – "look."

The radiator trickles heat into my naked feet. Except my toes, they only get the linoleum. 7:16 am always: the clock on the stove is busted. The morning sun dusts over the trees. Long cold lumps the air. No steam rises from the bowl of carbohydates on the metal table. The steam left minutes ago. Little red flakes of protein pool on top of the slop.

I nod, look down, can't speak, away from breakfast, check my feet, fiddling, letting them cool and reheat, waiting for her to shut up so I can eat.

"Teeth are seeds that sprout into new teeth. The more teeth the better," – she steps to the table and puts the tooth into my carbohydrates – "When you're bigger, the tooth fairy will come at night."

Her cigarette ashes to the filter in the ashtray on the countertop.

The morning isn't unrelated after all.

Dark. My bedsheets loosen. I carefully take out the tooth from the tooth fairy's pocket and hold it in my hand to warm it up. I hold it for a minute, put it in my mouth, then swallow. I fumble the fairy.

My eyes click and click and my teeth tickle. No sleep. None. Inside my eyelids: dirt holes: nausea. I slow my breath, black siphons into my mouth. All's I get is the taste of baking soda stuck between my teeth.

The sound of my father's phlegm cuts into my bedroom through the wall. A light switch snaps. He shuffles past my door.

Black creeps my bedroom. I wait a couple of minutes before I check under the pillow for the tooth fairy. I feel through the pillow, with the back of my head, for the soft lump of visitor. She's there. I reach under my pillow and hit a palm full of warm plastic. A fur heats fiber optic. I pull it out from under the pillow. A palm full of light. An animal. My animal nightlight, soft minus its three electrical prongs. I hold the animal in my hand for a few minutes, touching its belly, its bump of sun. The animal jerks slightly. It crawls down my arm, past my shoulder. Little claws prick into my bare skin.

The animal sprawls on my cheek and paws at my eyelashes, chews on them, not really hard. It rests on my left cheek, its belly becomes warmer and larger. Its belly breaks. Warm orange spills down my cheek and into my mouth, tastes of vitamins, unsweetened and acidic. A slight burn begins in the cracks of my lips and spreads to my cheek. A slight itch begins in the cracks of my lips and spreads to my cheek. My brain skits. I scratch my face: deep nail scoops to get it off. The animal bleeds somewhere in the sheets, the same orange blood that's under my nails, down my fingers, glows in the dark. I scratch and scratch and scratch. My cheek splits and spills down into my mouth, blood. The burning increases. I scream for my mom, but my screams only mix with hers, crawling through the drywall.

Scars

My hands slide to Preeti's hips, fingers between the scars on her lower back. Stretch marks more worm more thin more rough raised. My fingers snug perfectly between the ridges: a second ribcage reversed. Her breasts sag caged in black dreads. Soft panting happens. Streetlight scuttles up the wall in weak lymph. The dreads skim across my chest and again. I slide my hands away down her thighs, but she brings them back up, leans back. My cock bends inside her. I keep my hands on her hips, coma moist. She cums lukewarm against my groin. She shudders. Pubic hair is friction. I cum and tighten. Seeping happens. She slides off. She lies facing away from me. To the window: wall: wallpaper. Her back beads. Broken white branches on the blades: bubbles of blood ink: barbed needle. Her brown skin cuts white ink fuzz. The streetlight snags the undreaded hairs on her head: loose scalp sticks to the strands. I touch her hips, she shifts stiff. "What are these from?" I ask, rubbing the scars. Silence: lice: ice crystals on the corner of the window, a stalled crescent tall arched yellow. Low breaths then silence. "Myself," – she shifts to face me, her white teeth sharpened by dark – "my hips didn't grow evenly," – she rubs her side, ridges thick, adjusts the blanket. "Do you mind?" – I rub my thumb along the scars. "Sometimes, sometimes I don't. Depends," – she lies flat back against the mattress moving her jaw back and forth – "Mito-

23

sis is a bitch. Got any cloth?" She sits upright on the mattress, looking around the floor. "Should be," I say. I look around my side, around the ashtrays. A couple of scraps limp out under the mattress. I pull out two and hand them to her. She wipes her cunt and tosses them to the floor and gets back into bed. "What about your scars?" – her fingers poke my cheek.

"Long nails at night, when I was a kid, it was dark," I say. "Shit like that," – she shifts facing me and runs her nails through the two grooves on each side of my face – "happens at night, or even day, but especially night, they're ugly as hell". "Just like you, Rabe, just like you," I say. "Fuck," – she kicks me under the covers, her toenails gouge my shin – "you" – we laugh.

Still 1.10

Cobalt centres the room. A refrigerator rises: old General Electric cracks its handled chest open. Inside, 3 gratings: empty plastic jars all levels all lids gone. White powder cubes out over the lips. On the door side, cups dangle, plastic 2 from the top, 3 from the bottom. With nothing to eat, General Electric eats itself.

Carbon Cycle

Symptoms will not be described.

Secondary/opportunistic infections will not be described.

Stages will not be described.

Fluid levels will not be described.

Cell/viral load counts will not be described.

Words: sentences: narrative: dead lips can't bear stretch marks: can't describe disease or a slight case of singularity (DEATH) or much else for that matter.

Air tastes better when it's split. My syntax stinks acetone.

No description of the non-describes is possible because it will never match reality.

Besides the non-describes are not me because they are symptoms of me.

Microbes eat where they sleep where they shit where they fuck where they me.

Microbe me: they make me decay me carbon me cycle me nothing new.

Microbes are me. Disease is me. I am I saying I like I know what it is: changes every unit of whatever. Little room now for disease, the I disease. The I is dead the first time I leaked from my face. I makes ghosts of future mitosis. I is dead already, move on, only thing to be done. I am already a ghost ising: is is blunt is sharp is death is decay is entropy. See it work: how purdy like. I never was I from the cunt to the black. My disease doesn't really matter: call it X, Y, Z: don't matter much: all ends in the carbon cycle.

The best definition of post-man is this: a dildoing on two or more or less legs.

Language is disease is biotic is prophylactic is abiotic is cloud is plastic.

Cut your hand in a crowd and see what happens.

Still 1.02

A lily slurs in the open fist of a naked man I know named NO NAME
in front of a curtain stitched t-shirts ripped before sleep snows them
away. His cock is hard. This room has never seen heat or sunlight in
that order. Mercury or night or dust or cobalt in that order sift around
the curtain. Summer lyses open.

Pig

Belts parallel left and right stall along 1 jerk 2 pig screams every 12 seconds towards twin machine tubes. Pigs knuckle back, key into twin machine holes ass-out tail scabs bolt guns. Sputter scream and silence machines twist 90 degrees pigs spill onto parallel belts sputter red horizontal up the line chain tied to back hooves up on track knee broken gravity away.

"All great change in America starts at the inner table."

Pale flab vertical quarter cuts hang in rows of hundreds. Bleach ribs drips. Piss poor fluorescents standardize sway with the control of freezer logic. A man with hearing protection, eye protection, mouth protection, skin protection, smell protection, a grey hospital smock, and dirty boots sprays a garden hose walks up and down the aisle spine tight spraying scabs off the pavement. A second man with hearing protection, eye protection, mouth protection, skin protection, smell protection, a grey hospital smock, and dirty boots follows the first man down the aisle spine tight spraying scabs off him with a similar garden hose.

"Acts are stupid things – still born things, I should say."

Stuffed in rusted trucks, the pigs migraine in metre, blister to the floor. Outside the street is calm, no cars, afternoon garbage dust blows up through the gratings. Sniffing and snout all the things that make a good boy. Blue tags on the upper ears, infection bubbles most torn bitten off. Cobalt blue barcodes smear on their asses. A single pig sniffs and shits, inertia slams it and its shit to the left wall of the truck, squeals and sleep. Panel unbolts slides down in the back. An aluminum corridor hooks on.

"Freedom is never more than one generation dead. We didn't pass it to OUR brats in the bloodstream."

Soldered aluminum corridor: 3 metres by 5 metres by 20 metres. He wears hearing protection, eye protection, mouth protection, skin protection, smell protection, buttons a grid, tasers pigs running down the corridor.

"Technology is the oxygen of our modern age: it seeps through walls topped by freedom, it wafts across electrified bodies, to rust us from the inside-out."

HIV comes from the States in tiny foil packets we tear open with ourselves. Now HE sits on a hypodermic throne in our skulls clacking his glittered glued jawbone. He only gets off his lazy ass to come and see us 7 days a week, 365 days a year, screaming in burst balloons. Cold pale flares the machine, fire burns off the hair, blood, thought lands on the floor, more blood tumbles out back and forth, a man cuts the back vein on the pigs' legs. HIV, the deadbeat dad that isn't as deadbeat as I'd like.

"Life is one grand, sweetly scratched CD, so start the music."

In a back room, a woman who looks like Jackie O sharpens a knife with a machine, her gloves blue as California dirt. She loves the smell of friction: her eyes mouth it. Her brown bangs fall out of her hair net. She flips the knife and works the other side, starts with the inside, slides the handle back, sharpens the tip, curls, and flips the knife again. She repeats the same motion but pulling towards the left. She flips again and chews her tongue. She repeats the same cycle for 40 minutes because she has too. On the line, she cuts into the pig's esophagus or trachea, most likely both as they perform relatively the same function from an industrial angle but with different states of matter of which are also ultimately the same from an industrial angle. She cuts through the skin of the jaw, the snout, struck to the stillness, repeats the same movement for 6 hours encountering varying differences in the density of muscle and cuts made from previous machines.

"I have wondered at times what the Ten Commandments would have looked like if Moses had run them through a meat grinder?"

Metal building: 100m by 100m by 100m. 1 loading corridor North. 2 entrances East and West. 1 unloading arm South.

"Status quo, you know is Latin for 'the mess your body is.'"

I'm not sure where me and my parents got it from. I would like to say Reagan. My parents got it from a dead man and his sunset. They got it from Reagan. Who was part of They. They being them to put it dimly. This is not going to change much.

"How can a president not be an actor on reality television?"

Flames burn off the pig hair on a track around the ceiling shackles dark from the left pigs come in more back towards the flame chamber stragger inertia gravity into the fire. Sulphur dioxide. Out they come more paler water sprays drips the singe clean into and out the left sway pale flames strontium moisture vents water flares from the flame gets the last blood out. Stay on track. Nice to meat you, Reagan. Reagan and his 80s took turns fucking us: silence the only thing that trickles down ever. Reagan, he's been and will be every politician since himself: MITOSIS: SLOW DEATH. My mind bifurcates itself. A man vacuums the pig quarters with what looks like a Hoover from the USSR in the 70s if they were allowed to have them. CLOSED SYSTEM: OPEN SYSTEM. He does 36 pig quarters or 9 pigs in 8 minutes getting out all the shit from the former cavities melted plastic. I imagine. I like to imagine it was Reagan. There's a margin of hope here. A flabby margin of hope with tentative teeth. From the left, 1 pig comes in every 2 minutes, legs up, head down. A computer monitor with a circle saw extends its arms spreads the pig's legs arms spreads out the arms hugs all the way up grips the throat saws outwards and upwards towards the cock or cunt cuts into quarters. Pigs have cocks and cunts too.

"All the waste in a year from a nuclear power plant can be stored in my face."

Stomach bloats indigo stains itself to the intestines all strip out gravity doing what it does best skin splits intestines drop more or less the same rate anal beads bulbs of blue. Our technology is an evolutionary extension of ourselves. A bored, fat, stupid kid sits on a metal cylinder shaking hands with the quarters of pigs with hydraulic pincers. Cut hooves tumble down a black hole. No more descriptions of the hole: A hole is a hole is a hole.

"I've often said there's nothing better for the inside of a man than the insides and outsides of a pig."

Pig quarters on a conveyer belt grid-sawed, halved into eighths meet intestines and other tumble down a metal shoot MANGLED GROUND BURNED into white powder piles for the bagging. In all actuality it was Reagan. Or America. Or ourselves. Blaming ourselves, try that once. Rail that. Blame ourselves, not right. Blame America, not right. Blame Reagan, not right. But it will do. That'll do, pig. That'll do.

Commercial 1 – The Purple Cure

Last summer, I occupied a small cabin in one of the towns in the interior of American Columbia. To me it was a very boring and stupid town – partly because it was extremely boring and, partly, because it is known as a health resort. You live there hearing constantly the cough of the consumptive, and when you do meet an occasional American, he instantly begins discussing the condition of his bronchial tubes and forgets to inquire as to the state of your own lungs.

My lungs and bronchial tubes were perfectly soundless. I don't sleep and it wasn't for this that I sought the perfect repose and stillness of my coughing little town. I don't know why I came here. There was one American in this town, so I was told by someone I forget. And as I was assured that this American was phenomenally healthy and handsome, and was, moreover, a German, and hence presumably unable to converse with a boy wholly stupid of any knowledge of German or any other language, I didn't care that he was my next-door neighbor, beyond a floor of acorns. Two days after my arrival, I saw him digging in the dust bed behind his house and was struck by his singular resemblance to the portraits of Wernher von Braun. He looked seventy plus years old, he was skinny and boney, and his face, which had something of the harshness and liquidity of a sculpture made of Vaseline, was that of a man with perfect teeth and an indeterminate composition. I had already heard him called "the Cooker," this name doesn't really fit him. Absent thought and unremitting sun had reduced his clear-cut features. I made up my mind to avoid him, to not make his acquaintance. I could care less if he could speak English or use a stick or index finger with some dirt or even grunt.

Often during the first days of my residence next door to the American, I saw in the middle of the day a plastic bag slumped next to his dust patch and heard the huck of the spade. It is one of the advantages of not sleeping, that the patient can see in the night and day. What was the Cooker doing so early an hour in his dust? He could be gardening or ditching. Even an American philosopher would not be capable of getting up at one o'clock in the afternoon to plant starches or to improve the saturation of his garden because they are all dead. The only plausible explanation was that he was ditching. I resumed my sitting as I was sitting.

The bag situation solved itself later as it always does and proved to be edifying as the outcome was stupidly simple, since I didn't care about it at the time. The arrival at my neighbor's door of a jar of white rats and another of black rats, convinced me that he was engaged in studies, which involved the deaths of those happy little animals. Of course, when his white and black rats had died of unnatural causes, it became necessary to return them to the carbon cycle, and the Cooker coolly performed this task at midday in order to offer prejudices to curious people and to assert the fact that vivisection is merely a form of cutting shit up in which humans of the male variety now indulge purely for recreation. If his white and black rats were cut down, I hope they felt no boredom. I was unsure in the service of what human interest they died as we no longer have interests. I resumed my sitting as I was sitting.

My acquaintance with the Cooker – whom I will call Cooker Karms, for the reason that it was his name – grew awkwardly. We began by exchanging glances over the acorn floor, and I found he spoke English brokenly. We were both sloppy in our habits. We were both accustomed to standing in our dust patches every afternoon not moving. Gradually we passed from the discussion of silence to more interesting themes I'm sure, though I've forgotten what they were. And, finally, the Cooker accepted my invitation to come and inspect a flower growing under a floorboard, the name of which I was stupid of. He didn't know the name either. When I returned his visit, I accidently discovered that, unlike myself, he was a devotee of staring at me. That put a touch of parasitism on our acquaintance and we fell into the variable habit of him staring at me, every afternoon, from one to four.

· I found him extremely stupid. He was a doctor, though he had recently stopped practicing medicine in order to devote himself, so he told me, to the study of bio-engineering. He was a man of neither wide nor narrow culture, and he seemed to know nothing, which is also what charmed me in the man – nothing. His philosophy was not bounded by any of the limitations of color or greed. The sufferings of people may have touched him. His love for rats was mistakable, in spite of the fact that he buried his bag of rats. I had a dog, the dog walked around in front of my house, it was more or less my dog. Between the dog and Cooker Karms, a deep ambivalence sprang up. The man was neither happy nor unhappy when the dog sat by him and rested its skull on his leg: Karms simply emitted a constipated glow. Cooker Karms might have became severely attached to me. I understand why he lived so completely alone. When he tried explaining why he lives alone, I told him I already knew. He proceeded to tell me anyway. Gravely, he told me that a man should live for the benefit of the ones that pay you, and that his studies were more important than his pleasures. I called him stupid and returned home.

One night, my dog came into my cabin easily, as there were no doors, evidently feeling fine. He sniffed around and shat in his shitting corner. Karms came in too. He told me with imprecise hand gestures that the dog had shrunk to half of his ordinary size and he would soon not have the sufficient strength to forage, shit, screw, or drag himself away to die somewhere alone. My first thought was that Karms was being a drunken piece of shit. He rushed over to his house and came back with a baby blue bleach bottle, exhibiting little-to-no agitation. He walked to the dog and the dog backed away. The dog walked to him and Karms backed away. The dog and Karms walked equidistant to each other. The Cooker unscrewed the cap of the bleach bottle and poured it all over the dog, and then told me to wire into my Spade. I informed him I was already wired into it. He was silent for a moment or five. He told me to stand in the other room. I went and stood in other room. When I returned, he and the dog were missing. I went outside and noticed him in his dust patch beating the dust manically with blunt bottom of his shovel. I assumed he killed the dog, carefully removed the dog's body to his dust patch, and buried it, exercising the greatest care when touching it. He tossed his shovel into the woods, walked to me and informed me to wait in the room where the dog had initially been. He then went back to his house and I went back to mine. He returned with a large jar of gel that read GEL and a trowel and proceeded to disinfect the room and everything in it making meticulous horizontal strokes, with a chemical that caused a thick but entirely absent smell. When I asked him what was wrong with the dog he told me he ran away and I asked if he'd seen the dog digging in his dust. I didn't care what that dog dug up but I ascertained that the Cooker suspected that the dog disturbed his rat bags. While we waited for the gel to dissipate, he stared at me. The gel irritated my nasal passages. Karms went home. A new dog started foraging outside on the street that looked exactly like my last dog, only it was twice its size. I watched it consume abandoned buckets of rancid KFC. I assumed the food was rancid, as the dog started puking and shitting sulphur yellow and wiping its ass on the asphalt like it had worms.

I had been living next door to this Cooker for two weeks, when one evening his staring turned to a conversation on modes of resistance in late-market capitalism. The usual essay had just been published in Paris and I was expressing a good deal of ignorance at the artists, thinkers, *et al.* that did such a thing.

"The artist means well," said Cooker Karms, "but he is hopelessly stupid. He attacks the wrong people, and he uses absurdly inefficient weapons."

"What's an artist?" I asked him.

"Just what I say," he replied. "The artist wants to kill people who have money – post-capitalists, doctors, They, all who have money, power, life. These are the very people who are most necessary for the prolongation of life. If the artist tried to kill laboring or stagnated men, he would be working for the emancipation of the race from poverty, boredom, life."

"I hardly see myself anymore," I said. "Do you mean that the true way to ensure an artwork that lessons suffering in late-market capitalism is through the killing of the sufferers?"

"No, and yes," said Cooker Karms. "My dear friend, look at me. The poverty or incremental death of the lower socio-economic classes on this North America is the result of induced disease and a subsequent incremental perpetuation of existence and a saturation of choice and benefits given by They. They is just a variable, remember, that represents the ambiguous Foucauldian power structures and elites that control. Why does a poor North American sit at home doing nothing, and spend his whole life in a state of incremental death? Because They give him the means to do so with perfect care, food, clothing, shelter."

"This might be a stupid question, but why doesn't They just kill us?" I asked.

"That is a stupid question. Because humans don't kill or do anything directly anymore. Mass extermination is no longer a feasible option, but its equal and opposite suits the same end quite well, that being mass perpetuation. Death spread over a lifetime incrementally is still death."

"That sounds highly mathematical," I said, "but I haven't been taught any confidence in figures. They have kept me in an intellectual stasis indefinitely."

"Any person who sees things as they are sees," continued the Cooker, disregarding my previous insight, "that the world is perfectly under-populated. If a mutated HIV virus or some other disease, doesn't matter, swept off four-sixths of the remaining population of North America, it would be even better. Now, the artists don't see this. They would kill off They – the very people who give the means to live comfortably. I, on the contrary, would not harm the ones who pay me, but I would continue this fatal under-population – an eventuality that grows warmer and warmer every year. Our American Malthus can't glimpse what is coming because he is dead."

"I'm bored. I don't care anymore. Where's my Atari?" I said.

"Yes. Did I not tell you the remedy is to continue the decrease in population? The person who discovers how to do this would be the greatest benefactor They have ever known."

It bored me to hear this man whom I knew to be a creep and weird-hearted actually insisting that about two-fourths of the population of the globe ought to be, I'm not sure for the sake of They, but I thought little about it at the time. I knew how fond men and women equally are of propounding crazy and anti-altruistic theories which they themselves dream of carrying into action and in turn into a reality. Here was a man whose duty it may have been to stare at the sick and so to prolong the existence of the weakest classes for They. It was another illustration of the inevitable tongue which, sooner or later, licks the asshole of every scientific man.

Have I said that Karms lived completely alone? One afternoon the Cooker did not appear to be staring at me from his dust beds, and in the evening, he did not come as usual into my cabin. Suspecting he was dead and curious as to what I could steal from him, I walked to a window of his cabin where I guessed his room to be and called to him. He answered by coughing. His head propped up and he opened the window. He said he was quite well, but he was not able to stare at me until the next day. I went back to my cabin feeling somewhat easy, and considered breaking into his house the next morning to kill him in case he refused to open the door.

When I called at his cabin the next afternoon, he opened the door and stared at me for three minutes. He was looking wretchedly sleep-deprived, but he assured me that his whatever was over. He took me into his living room and I was not surprised by the sterility of it. The carpet was perfectly grey. There was a television and a radio placed on the table connected to a banister which extended six metres to the ceiling. In front of the banister was a simple armchair, vertical lined yellow brown gold. There was a three-panel wooden coffee table with a book on the far right panel that never opened. The brown leather couch behind it didn't depress at all. The fireplace was stupid: a quad-rant of a circle made of rectangular stone. Beside the fireplace, there was a table with a red and black vase grafted to it. Across the room, there was a glass table with five chairs that didn't move. There was a bookshelf filled with what looked like psychology books. Outside the vast windows was a painted skyline of Seattle. There was white and brown dog hair over everything for some reason.

In his living room, he tried to converse with me with his usual unease. The attempt was as usual a failure, and I saw that, besides being shakey from the effect of his whatever that had happened, his eyes looked fat.

His eyes remained fat where he stood scratching his arm for a while, and then said:

"My dear friend, I want to apologize for yesterday's hermitage, but on that very morning both Ed, my dog, and Nills, my fuck buddy, passed. My dear friend, I don't trust you. But I'm going to die sud-denly and soon too. Death is contagious, you know. Their deaths have shown me that at the edge of the abyss, the silence is so deafening that death doesn't exist. In case that I might die, a scenario that will happen shortly, there must be someone who will know how to pre-vent the catastrophe which would happen to They's pretty big world, where I have accumulated for them so much expended human capital. Give me a word that what I'm going to tell you won't leave that sexy skull so long as you live."

"No," I said to him rashly, then, I asked him frankly what he wanted to tell me.

He stared at me for three minutes, then asked me to follow him to his bathroom. The bathroom wasn't less a room than a labyrinth of glass tubing, Pyrex dishes, glass bottles, plastic bottles, toilet paper, thermometres, ripped t-shirts, plastic funnels, broken blenders, yellow rubber gloves, a spade, yellow rubber tubing, clear plastic tubing, plastic pails, canisters of propane (19lb), tape, c-clamps, spiral bound notebooks, a "Microorganisms for Dummies" book, hotplates, aluminum foil, a laptop, cardboard boxes, trays, trademarked glass vials, cologne sample vials, trays with glass vials in them, a mini-fridge, measuring cups, curtains, broken beakers, Isopropyl, Toluene, Ether, Sulphuric Acid, Red Phosphorus, salt, a dead dog, Lithium, Trichloroethane, Sodium, Anhydrous Ammonia, Sodium Hydrochloride, dried saliva, Pseudoephedrine, Ephedrine, dried semen, nail polish, sawdust.

There was nothing interesting about the bathroom. I had once before seen a picture of a laboratory in an old magazine and it didn't seem at all like it. Under the counter, behind a missing cupboard door, was a shoebox filled with one-inch long glass vials with plastic stoppers, containing what I assumed to be liquid crystal meth. Karms nodded to these and said:

"When I die someday soon, I want you to take all these vials, break them in one of these yonder plastic buckets or flush them down the toilet."

"I will," I said. "You're the doctor. The vials, I presume, contain samples of various liquid methamphetamines?"

His eyes tightened up with the fat of violence. "They contain the uncells that cure the world's most deadly diseases, notably HIV and cancer," he mumbled. "They are all young. I engineered them myself and they are more beneficial than any treatment approved by the medical profession since it no longer exists. You remember the death of that stray dog? I killed him in a fit of joy after discovering the cure for HIV that I engineered actually works. If that cure were once introduced into North America, it would spread so rapidly that in eight to ten business days, the continent would be repopulated."

"I'm stupid. I don't understand what you mean by cures. How is it possible for man to invent a cure?"

"I keep forgetting you're stupid. Lie down on the floor," – he sat down on the toilet and I stretched out on the bathroom floor, – "Certain cures are produced by certain cells or uncells that have had their DNA tinkered with by certain bioengineers who reprogram the information within them to turn them into organic machines to hunt down the diseases. Reverse engineering is easier than actual."

"You engineer in this space?" I ask.

"Reverse," he says. "Yes. Look at this vial labeled HOPE 8. It contains the cure for most types of cancer. Administered to a patient, it cures in four hours. I have tried to mix different cures together to get new and better cures, but I only get noise. It was I who invented the cure for influenza. You remember influenza, don't you?"

"No," I say.

"Anyway, I was living in St. Pittsburg and while walking one day, the vial for it, I forget the label name, fell out of my pocket. To this day, I have never seen a case of it. Someone probably railed it. Look at this tube labelled HOPE 13. It contains the uncells that cures herpihila and dropsyche. If this cure got out, it would certainly be very infectious, should it ever get epidemic. However, I have invented other cures that fuck it in the ass. Here is a vial labelled HOPE 1," he continued, taking it hatingly in his hand, "which contains my *plus grande fuck up*. The uncells are a cross between HIV-1, HIV-2, and that pesky SIV all cofucked together in a botched simian sperm. Making sense? (I stared in the sink clogged with matchsticks.) Good. I call this cure, which all this crossed shit produces the "Purple Cure," for no reason.

It cures in less than 30 seconds and there is no strain of HIV that can screw with it. As to its infectious nature, it is the They of all cures. If I were to crack this vial open and drain it down your throat, you would be cured within a minute. You would then go and fuck someone else and give it to them in the blood. Then this fuck would fuck another fuck and this fuck would fuck another fuck, amplifying the Cure until the whole world is infected. If I were to toss the contents of this vial into the air, the inflection would gyrate so motilely that in two minutes, every non-They would be cured in this poor little shithole. Think what would happen if a single pipe bomb made of cotton gauze or some other reasonable, lower socio-economic substitute saturated with the Purple Cure was detonated in your AIDS ghetto. In six minutes, there would be two million survivors!"

The man's canine teeth sparked with spit. His weirdness had premeditatedly ceased while he silenced, but suddenly he sank back on the toilet and valiantly asked me to blow him. I refused.

After he finished jerking off on the toilet and had somewhat regained something, I asked him why he even created the fucking thing in the first place, if it's so detrimental to They's control and society.

"To destroy it," he said, scraping his jism off his belly with a microscope slide, "and make its destruction a reality now and foreverish. Waste. Artful waste. Superfine waste," he looked up to the ceiling and muttered something at a conveniently placed water stain with the perfect symmetry of a halo, then looked back at me, "I already fucking told you," he screamed, "that I'm an ARTIST, only unlike other artists, I have SOPHISTICATED STUPIDITY! You have heard me say all the boredom and poverty are the results of modern technological living. I'm just repeating this. By destroying the Cure, I'm helping the people that pay me and humanity as a side effect. Imagine for one second if I actually infected the population of your ghetto with the Cure. The lower classes would be cured and turn into workmen and demand wages to permit them to fuck, eat, shit and die in brilliant luxury, a likes only They have ever seen because They currently live

44

in it. Besides, They have other means and unseen diseases at their disposal also: They always do. Why am I explicating right now!? I told you artists select the wrong victims and that their art is just stupid!"

I stood there in his bathroom. A plastic bottle of Isopropyl fell somewhere in the tangle.

His face started up again –

"I don't want my ART to fall into bodies that would use them productively. That's not why I've asked you here today. I just wanted you to verify it, that's all. I'm quite able to destroy it and die by myself, I've already started a fire before you came." He then took the vial and swallowed it. The house hazed up. He let himself fall backward into the mess, then back stoked around a bunch to get tangled in the glass and tubing, then hugged one of the 19lb canisters of propane. I tried to pull him out but he was ratted in but good. The smoke became thicker so I left. There were the usual flames, the usual gropings, the usual sounds of collapse, the usual explosions.

The Cooker's cabin was burned stiff in twenty-four hours. The dog, the new one, and I sat equidistant and watched it smolder, the former trying occasionally to lick the latter. No one else in the town noticed the fire. The rusted trucks roared past without a single stop or honk or spit from the drivers. The sides of my cabin were melted and smelled of white phosphorous. After the last smoke of the pile, the dog and I triangulated the bathroom, found the Cooker's body: bruised ashes meshed dust: a thigh and metal: his face blue skull half-melded with a shredded propane canister. We had a moment of something for his passing, the dog took a shit and I poked the Cooker's body with a charred cookie pan. After the moment, the clouds cruxed themselves over the trees dirt black, so we went in to my cabin and watched for rain. It never came, so we sat on the carpet and dozed off.

The next morning, I left that cabin with my bag. I left the dog there because it wanted to sniff still. I can't even remember what that cabin looked like. While hitching back east, I walked upon a torched gas station, and met with an incendiary named Axel, who claimed to be a horse thief and biologist. I asked him how long uncells closed in a vial containing some sort of sharp gel that resembled meth would be able to remain viable in the esophagus and/or stomach of someone that was burned alive. His answer was, "Maybe." That answer did something to my life. Three inches off the ground, in the burned cabin of Cooker Karms, sits the Purple Cure in possible stasis until the morning when that forest will share the same fate as all forests to be cut and levelled to make way for cellphone towers. Then the vial will crack and the Cure will motile away. This will happen: entropy. I have often thought of breaking the vial myself, but I'm bored, tired, and forgotten where the place is and my spade can't recreate that place anymore.

OK. Fuck you, where's my Atari?

Food 1.1

Four hands stacked, four hands fat holds a clear bowl in front of my face. The ladle drops a dollop of melted Vaseline, ripples up the curves, loosens steam. "Dollop," a he says. The ladle pulls up. Above, a hand cracks a white packet of white salt in the middle of the bowl, ripples the surface. The hand cracked packet pulls up. A half sphere of yellow in the middle. Clear gel still circles on the outside. "Enough," says another he. Red rectangles flutter down, some stick to the sides of the bowl and clot. "Dab," another he says. Some rectangles ripple the liquid and spider red to the bottom of the bowl. "Poke," a she says. Her fingers powdered blue grid the surface and clot. "Morning," the she says. All four people slowly back up and out the room. The bowl wobbles on my stomach.

Linoleum

Preeti gets up off the mattress, hugs a red blanket around her, her dreads meld in with the frayed yarn, steps to the window straight ahead, pulls the blue towel hung on a rod to the left side, looks down at the street, then sways back and forth, the blanket falls to under her shoulder blades. The sunlight blackens the acne scars on her temples and shoulders. The sun almost comes over the building across the street. Pigeon cries cut the silence, but there are no pigeons. Little strings blow off the top of a single dirt pile on the floor, left of the bed. The door is half-open. There might be a breeze from the kitchen.

"I don't want to do anything today," I say. "Are you sure?" she says. "Doesn't matter, what is there to do?" I say. "You are being stupid, lots to do," she says. She half-turns and picks the dirt from underneath the nails of her right hand with her left thumbnail. The dirt collects under the new nail. She wipes a single line in the dust across the width of the window frame. "You are being stupid," she says. She leaves the window, walks left to the doorframe and starts to toe pick at the curling linoleum. "Even this shit gets up more than you do, in your next life you're going to be linoleum," she says. "Not bad," I say. "Ask the linoleum that," she says, "all the shit it has put up with." She laughs in a shrill tone for a minute: all her missing molars gauge out. I still haven't gotten used to the laugh. She crouches down and pulls at a curling edge of the linoleum. She tugs up two squares and tosses them at me, landing on my feet under the sheet. "I can't reach that far," I say. "I forgot, what I was laughing at," she says. "The linoleum," I say. "I forgot what, I was laughing at," she says. I pick at the wallpaper: it doesn't let me pick it. "What do you want to do today," she says. "Nothing," I say. "Maybe or not," she says. "Don't know," I say. "You don't know because," she says. "Don't know, not your fault, just don't know," I say. "You could fuck me again," she says. "No," I say. "Or I could fuck you again," she says. "No," I say. The pile of dust in the middle of the room has doubled in size. More strings fall off the top. She goes back to the window, reaches and picks a little corner of the wallpaper, and pulls it down, a perfect rectangle, curls it up into a cig roll, and starts fraying the edges into a circle. After she's finished, she rests it on the window frame. "What are you making," I say. "I don't know," she says. She picks another corner, pulls another strip of wallpaper, same perfect rectangle. "You know, you have to do something, anything, you just fucking sit there like you're already grounded, soaking up dust, quit being fucking stupid, you can do anything," she says and continues to gently fray the edges of the little wallpaper roll. She places the second roll on the frame next to the other one. She bends down, rubs the dried skin off her legs. "What do you want to do today," she says. She bends down, rubs the dried skin off her legs. "Nothing," I say. She bends down, rubs the dried skin off her legs. "Aren't you going to ask if I've fucked any one new?" she says. "No," I say. "Aren't you going to ask if I have the Cure yet?" she says. "No," I say. "What do you want me to do today," she says. "Rip off all the wallpaper, it dies or I do," I say. "You're a lemon," she says. "What's a lemon," I say. "I don't know," she says. She starts ripping another rectangle of wallpaper. The sun almost comes over the building across the street.

School

but not, up the street, from the house, two minute walk. School is the word used because it is the closest one but not at all since no one remembers what it means: parents almost remember what school was if not at all: school is school but not. School but not is a fallen strip mall: five blocks by two blocks: half of it an old supermarket: a metal hole: I-beams upon I-beams upon I-beams, sharp, bent, rusted or dull: birds, mice, nests of chewed pink insulation: stock piles of pornography and something called "Paradise Lost" that nobody can or wants to read, people only use it to wipe their asses with: cans, old, empty, flat, sharp, full, botulism out the sides: fluorescent tubes broken, tube shards, shards, less than shard, dust, less than dust: light sockets, straight down, tilted: banisters: railings: carpet, ripped, black and white, shit or puke or blood-stained: old conveyer belts: shelves: metal carts: ceiling fans, straight down, tilted: tiles: meat hooks: VHS tapes, broken, gutted, melted: jugs of insecticide, bleach, soda, other: dry wall chunked, half-up: fire pits: darkness.

 Three floors of collapse: top, middle, down, linked by one stairwell, the central support column. I walk down to the bottom, tap the steps, fake steps mashed porn, fall deep, traps for. Each stair of silent eyes and tits and footprints stares up. At the bottom, two fire pits flare up front, two flare at back: thick plastic smoke. I wait at the bottom letting my eyes adjust to the metal. Fluorescent tubes twist above into ceiling fans. Every couple of steps I bend medium-to-low. Mobiles of coat hangers, meat hooks, and pornography sway in the dark suspended with cable upwards. I walk back to one of the fires in the back and sit on a overturned metal locker, screws buckle, metal sags under my weight. Across the fire, a shadow jerks off orange and black, can tell from the noises. Another shadow less shadow now than the other stoops by the fire. It holds a coat hanger into the fire burning a mouse stinking of bleach. We sit silent: only the crackle of mouse and rustle of zipper can be heard. The shadow closest turns its head: freckles, missing teeth, dirt and orange curls into a boy: "Hey wanna try," he says. "Just ate," I say. "You gotta try," he says. The freckles cast shadows up his face, missing all four top front teeth, bottoms perfectly straight and black. "Here," he says. He passes the coat hanger with a bowie knife handle. I take a bite of the mouse, the skin slides off, prickles of black, steam pink underneath, little tough lumps, some bone as I chew, spit the hard shit back into the fire. "Good, huh," he says. "Alright," I say. We laugh. He steps back and sits on the locker, screws buckle, the metal sags further. "Check this," he says, shows me the handle. "Did it myself, found it, stuck the wire in, melted it a bit." I don't know his name. I call him Red. He hands it to me, the handle warm from the heat. "Red," he says. "Elliott," I say. Red strips off the remaining meat with his hand and eats it. He tosses the bones into the fire and rests the hanger into it. Smoke rises into the rafters: orange webs into the I-beams. "Perfect," he says, spits more bones and bits of hard into the fire. He moves closer on the locker. After he's done, he wipes his fingers on my knees. We laugh. The grease around his lips glistens in the firelight. "Catch," a voice says across the fire. A phone ripped sharp cord arcs the dark fire hits my chest: grease on the handle glowing black. The shadow laughs. "It's for you," the shadow says, laughs again. The grease stinks of copper. The shadow keeps laughing. Red grabs the hanger, circles right around the fire and whips the shadow's head. It screams, rolls around in the metal dirt. I grab the phone cord, circle right around the fire, whip, aiming for its teeth: the only white in the mess. It screams again. Red whips: I whip: we don't stop until the white in the teeth screams black too. I toss the phone into a pile of metal. Red puts the hanger back in the fire. We sit back on the locker, right hands glistening with black. Red licks the black blots around his lips. I lick my lips too. We shake and breathe through the nose, sit in the crackles. Steps scratch in the metal overhead: dust falls. Red holds my hand. His nails long thin zipper my palm. My hand lightens in the hold. We watch the lumped shadow for minutes watching for a tick. "Let's get out," he says. "Just leave?" I say. "That?" he says, points to the fire. "Yeah," I say. "Yeah," he says. Red takes the hanger out of the fire, walks right and whips the shadow's head until he's out of breath. I get up walk round left and give one last boot to what I think is its head. Red jams the hanger down one of its face hole: the bowie handle dangles in the orange. We let our eyes adjust to the metal, then walk up the stairwell, holding hands, testing the steps.

St. Nowhere

Six levels, basement to top. They start you off at the top, work your way down. Or start you off at the bottom and work your way up. Or leave you where you start. All the same. Level five is the current level. It doesn't matter which level They house me. Each of the six floors is circular as circular can be with six sides. Squarely circular. Each of the six sides divides at the middle into two rooms making twelve rooms on each level. Each of the twelve rooms narrows either to the right or to the left, depending on the side of the dividing wall it falls on. In the center of each level, a room contains four desks facing North, East, South and West closed in by six glass walls. The North desk faces rooms 5L and 5A with rooms 5J, 5K, 5B and 5C on the periphery. The East desk faces rooms 5C and 5D with rooms 5A, 5B, 5E and 5F on the periphery. The South desk faces rooms 5F and 5G with rooms 5D, 5E, 5H and 5I on the periphery. The West desk faces rooms 5I and 5J with rooms 5G, 5H, 5K and 5L on the periphery. Level five is the current level. It doesn't matter which level They house me. This has been mentioned previously. Four people either Somebodies or Nobodies can watch from the desks. The Nobodies have no bodies. The Somebodies have some body. Usually there are four Somebodies or three Somebodies and a Nobody or two Somebodies and two Nobodies or one Somebody and three Nobodies or four Nobodies. The more Nobodies there are, the less the Somebodies turn their heads therefore covering less distance visually. If there are four Nobodies, each has a visual field of 90 degrees. If there is only one Somebody at any one of the desks and three Nobodies in the remaining three, the Somebody's field of vision is only 60 degrees leaving the Nobodies' field of vision 100 degrees each. If there are two Nobodies and two Somebodies sitting opposite, back-to-back, or perpendicular to one another, each has a 55 degree visual field, leaving the Nobodies with a field of 125 degrees each. If there are three Somebodies and one Nobody, each Somebody has a field of vision of 50 degrees, leaving the Nobody with a field of vision of 210 degrees. When all four desks are filled with Somebodies, each has a field of vision of only 20 degrees, leaving 280 degrees unaccounted for. There is nothing to account for this loss. The carpet outside is red and worn down around the glass. The floor smells of bleach. The temperature is 12 degrees Celsius. At this temperature, the flies cannot operate and either die or roll around on the carpet or consolidate in the six corners or play torpor accordingly. The door of my room narrows to the right. The resident on the other side of the wall that complements me in some touching yet meaningless way, remains unknown. Attempts have been made to see the other residents of the floor. The attempts prove difficult as They neither enable nor encourage me to leave the room. 5K is the current room. 5K narrows to the right. The room They house me in is erroneous. From my room, moving counter-clockwise, floral print wallpaper with vertical bands comes into view. Room 5J slides into view from the left. The door is closed, on the left are two piles of dishes, one of bowls and one of glass cups. The bowls are stacked one on top of another. The cups are stacked one inside the other, compounding the glass and light. On the right side of the door is a pile of bedsheets that are known as bedsheets because they are what partially enclose me. They might be curtains. A clean bedpan sits on top. The bedpan is assumed clean because one similar to it catches my shit frequently. The shit is easy to ascertain. The door is white. The knob twists to the left and to the right and stops. Under the door shine two bars of light, divided by a black void. The bar on the left enlarges as the bar on the right recedes. The bar on the right enlarges as the bar on the left recedes. The void fades leaving a solid bar of light under the door. The door slides to the right. Ripped wallpaper comes into view, floral with vertical bands. Room 5I slides into view from the left. The door is white and slightly open with a continuous bar of blue light under the door, then up the vertical edge, then on the horizontal top. The sound of a fan comes from the room. The room smells of television static. There is nothing on the floor on either side of the doorframe. The doorframe slides to the right. Ripped wallpaper, narrow strips at the top, wide at the bottom, comes into view. On the carpet, below the wide tear of wallpaper, a kettle boils plugged into a socket. The steam rises and disappears as all steam does. There are no cups. The kettle slides to the right. Room 5H slides into view from the left. The door is less white than the other doors. Paint or light might account for this difference. It is neither the paint nor the light. The door is the same white. The door slides to the right. Wallpaper, the same floral pattern with vertical bands, and a fire alarm slides into view from the left. An outline of a fire extinguisher sits directly under the alarm. The wallpaper within the outline is brighter than the surrounding wallpaper. Room 5G slides into view from the left. The door is open. Inside, the room widens to the right. The walls, floor, bed, windows, cabinet, closet, ceiling, and bed stand are all white. A Spade is on the bed stand. The Spade blends with the wall. The room smells of antibiotic piss. The door moves to the right. Floral wallpaper slides into view from the left. Room 5F slides into view from the left. A man in a large, dark blue work suit smears a clear gel over the door with a clear plastic trowel. The man is average height and build with a large patch of hair missing from the back of his skull. Eczema covers the backs of his ears. Eczema covers the sides of his cheeks. Eczema covers the back of his neck. Eczema covers the backs of his hands. Eczema covers his wrists. Eczema covers his forearms. Eczema does not cover his

57

elbows. He reaches down to a large jar of the gel on the carpet with an opening just big enough for the trowel. The jar is half-empty. The label on the jar reads GEL. He doesn't shift his head backward, forward, or to the side. The man bends down with his back straight and skims the gel from the jar. The man smears it horizontally, three smears down from the top of the doorframe. By the eleventh smear from the top, he is halfway done. The jar by his left ankle is three-quarters empty. After the twenty-first smear, the door is sealed. The first smear on the top evaporates. The man bends down with his back straight not moving his head backward, forward, or to the side. He picks up the lid hidden behind the jar and screws it on. The man picks up the jar and stands up. He holds the jar in one hand and shuffles to the right facing forward. The third smear from the top evaporates. The doorframe slides to the right after the seventh smear from the top evaporates. Wallpaper slides into view from the left. The wallpaper is increasingly ripped. This is good. Room 5E slides into view from the left. The door is closed. There are no piles outside the door. Behind the door, two people talk. Two people are talking. One person talks while the other listens. The listening is indicated by a silence. The talking is indicated by warbling. That is the sound of talking. One warbles while the other silences. The roles may inverse. Above the door, an overhead fan doesn't turn. A single black void slides under the door from the left to the right. The doorframe slides to the right. There is wallpaper. Room 5D slides into view from the left. The room is not a room. Inside, two stalls extend left. On each of the stalls there is a pale curtain that adheres to the sides and the top pole. A rusted wheelchair waits outside of each stall. The floor is made of red tiles. That color is exact. Black sealant lines the tiles. This is wrong. Mildew lines the tiles. Drips are heard. Both showerheads may drip. Or the closest showerhead drips while the farthest remains closed. Or the farthest showerhead drips while the closest remains closed. Or the drips emanate from an unseen pipe. The source of the drip is tiresome. A discharge of water leaks from one of the showerheads. The exact showerhead that facilitated the discharge is not identified. The water pools down to a single drain clogged with pubic hair and gauze. The doorframe slides to the right. Wallpaper slides to the right. Drywall deposits the texture of acne slide to the right. Horizontal bands of gel slides to the right. Gel covers the doorframe. Room 5C slides into view from the left. The gelatinous doorframe slides to the right. Drywall saturated with gel slides to the right. Room 5B slides into view from the left. A man in a large, dark blue work suit smears a clear gel over the door with a clear plastic trowel. The man is average height and build with a large patch of hair missing from the back of his skull. Eczema covers the backs of his ears. Eczema covers the sides of his cheeks. Eczema covers the back of his neck. Eczema covers the backs of his hands. Eczema covers his wrists. Eczema covers his forearms. Eczema covers his elbows. When he reaches up, his pants shift accordingly, revealing eczema-covered ankles. He reaches down to a large jar of the gel on the carpet with an opening just big enough for the trowel. The jar is half-empty. The label on the jar reads GEL. He doesn't shift his head backward, forward, or to the side. The man bends down with his back straight and skims the gel from the jar. The man smears it horizontally three smears down from the top of the doorframe. By the eleventh smear from the top, he is halfway done. The jar by his left ankle is three-quarters empty. After the twenty-first smear, the door is sealed. The first smear on the top evaporates. The man bends down with his back straight not moving his head backward, forward, or to the side. He picks up the lid behind the jar and screws it on. The man picks up the jar and stands up. He holds the jar in one hand and shuffles to the left facing forward. The third smear from the top has evaporated. The doorframe slides to the left in time to the steps of the man. The man faces forward, steps three times, and stops. He puts down the jar, carefully unscrews the lid, placing it in front of the jar, hidden out of view. There is no wallpaper on the wall. He dips the trowel into the jar, stands up and starts to spread the gel on the wall from the top and across. He produces two horizontal bands for every trowel of gel. The man has smeared six bands when he starts to shift to the right. Room 5A slides into view from the left. The door shuts. A single black void under the door wavers in the centre, grows lighter, then moves to the right then disappears. To the right of the door, a large stack of glass cups teeters in a single, metallic bedpan. The bedpan is full of shit and piss. The shit and piss pool over the lip of the bedpan and spill onto the carpet. From the right, the man shuffles into view one leg at a time with his trowel in his left hand and the jar of gel in the right. He looks forward. He shuffles until his left foot stops next to the bedpan. The soles of his shoe depress the carpet, causing the piss and shit to spill and pool under his foot. He bends down, puts the jar of gel by his right foot, unscrews the top, and places the lid in front of the jar, hidden out of view. The jar is half-empty. He takes the trowel and dips it into the jar, then stands up and begins to cover the door with the gel starting at the top. The man and the door slide to the right. The walls are bare. The carpet is worn. Room 5L slides into view from the left. The door is closed. Nothing is stacked. The door slides to the right. Room 5K slides into view from the left. The door has already been described. The door has not been described. Nothing is stacked outside the door. End.

PIT

The room darkens. A lightbulb descends from the ceiling above the origin in the centre of the floor. Somebody 1 enters the room, lies down, at the origin, erection vertically upwards. Somebody 1 fans its legs and arms in a circle. The average lengths of its fans are 1 metre: the radius of the circle created is 1 metre. Quadrants glow. Quadrant 2: a metre up to the door, $\pi/2$, counterclockwise right angle a metre to the wall on the left, π. Quadrant 3: a metre to wall, π, counterclockwise right angle a metre to the foot of the bed, $3\pi/2$. Quadrant 4: a metre to the foot of the bed, $3\pi/2$, counterclockwise right angle a metre to the window on the right, 2π. Quadrant 1: a metre to the window on the right, 2π, counterclockwise right angle a metre up to the door, $\pi/2$. Preeti enters the room naked, walks to the origin, bends down, inserts Somebody 1's erection into her anus and superimposes herself over its body. Both their left hands fall at $\pi/4$. Both their right hands fall at $3\pi/4$. Both their left ankles fall at $7\pi/4$. Both their right ankles fall at $5\pi/4$. Five more Somebodies enter the room. The Somebodies are Somebodies 2 through 6. Somebodies 2 through 6 hold their erections. Somebodies 3 through 6 carry straight razors. Somebody 2 assumes $\pi/2$. Somebody 3 assumes $3\pi/4$. Somebody 4 assumes $5\pi/4$. Somebody 5 assumes $7\pi/4$. Somebody 6 assumes $\pi/4$. Somebody 2 lies down, inserts its erection into Preeti's mouth, and rests its mouth on her vagina, its head at the origin. Somebodies 3 through 6 reach down, hold Preeti's limb that corresponds with their position and make a medium subdermal incision where the skin will allow. The incisions are made with the grain of the skin between the epidermis and dermis but not the hypodermis. On each of Preeti's limbs, a small pocket is made. After the pockets are made, Somebodies 3 through 6 insert the tips of their erections into the pocket. The system begins. The usual groans. The usual moans. The usual screams. The system slows. Somebody 2 raises itself, removes its erection from Preeti's mouth, crawls back upright at $\pi/2$. Somebodies 3 through 6 remove their erections from the respective limbs. Somebodies 2 through 6 shift positions. Somebody 2 shifts to $3\pi/4$. Somebody 3 shifts to $5\pi/4$. Somebody 4 shifts to $7\pi/4$. Somebody 5 shifts to $\pi/4$. Somebody 6 shifts to $\pi/2$. Somebody 6 lies down, inserts its erection into Preeti's mouth, and rests its mouth on her vagina, its head at the origin. Somebodies 2 through 5 reach down, hold Preeti's limb that corresponds with their position, and insert the tips of their erections into the pockets. The system begins. The usual groans. The usual moans. The usual screams. The system slows. Somebody 6 raises itself, removes its erection from Preeti's mouth, crawls back upright at $\pi/2$. Somebodies 2 through 5 remove their erections from the respective limb. Somebodies 2 through 6 shift positions. Somebody 2 shifts to $5\pi/4$. Somebody 3 shifts to $7\pi/4$. Somebody 4 shifts to $\pi/4$. Somebody 5 shifts to $\pi/2$. Somebody 6 shifts to $3\pi/4$. Somebody 5 lies down, inserts its erection into Preeti's mouth, and rests its mouth on her vagina, its head at the origin. Somebodies 2 through 4 and 6 reach down, hold Preeti's limb that corresponds with their position, and insert the tips of their erections into the pockets. The system begins. The usual groans. The usual moans. The usual screams. The system slows. Somebody 5 raises itself, removes its erection from Preeti's mouth, crawls back upright at $\pi/2$. Somebodies 2 through 4 and 6 remove their erections from the respective limb. Somebodies 2 through 6 shift positions. Somebody 2 shifts to $7\pi/4$. Somebody 3 shifts to π/4. Somebody 4 shifts to π/2. Somebody 5 shifts to 3π/4. Somebody 6 shifts to 5π/4. Somebody 4 lies down, inserts its erection into Preeti's mouth, and rests its mouth on her vagina, its head at the origin. Somebodies 2 and 3 and 5 and 6 reach down, hold Preeti's limb that corresponds with their position, and insert the tips of their erections into the pockets. The system begins. The usual groans. The usual moans. The usual screams. The system slows. Somebody 4 raises itself, removes its erection from Preeti's mouth, crawls back upright at π/2. Somebodies 2 and 3 and 5 and 6 remove their erections from the respective limb. Somebodies 2 through 6 shift positions. Somebody 2 shifts to π/4. Somebody 3 shifts to π/2. Somebody 4 shifts to 3π/4. Somebody 5 shifts to 5π/4. Somebody 6 shifts to 7π/4. Somebody 3 lies down, inserts its erection into Preeti's mouth, and rests its mouth on her vagina, its head at the origin. Somebodies 2 and 4 through 6 reach down, hold Preeti's limb that corresponds with their position, and insert the tips of their erections into the pockets. The system begins. The usual groans. The usual moans. The usual screams. The system slows. Somebody 3 raises itself, removes its erection from Preeti's mouth, crawls back upright at π/2. Somebodies 2 and 4 through 6 remove their erections from the respective limb. Somebodies 2 through 6 shift positions. Somebody 2 shifts to π/2. Somebody 3 shifts to 3π/4. Somebody 4 shifts to 5π/4. Somebody 5 shifts to 7π/4. Somebody 6 shifts to π/4. Somebody 2 lies down, inserts its erection into Preeti's mouth, and rests its mouth on her vagina, its head at the origin. Somebodies 3 through 6 reach down, hold Preeti's limb that corresponds with their position, and insert the tips of their erections into the pockets. The system begins. The usual groans. The usual moans. The usual screams. The usual discharge. The system slows. Somebody 2 raises itself, removes its erection from Preeti's mouth, crawls back upright at π/2. Somebodies 3 through 6 remove their erections from the respective limbs. Somebodies 2 through 6 leave the room. Somebody 1 removes its erection from Preeti's anus. Somebody 1 slides out from under Preeti, stands at π/2. Somebody 1 leaves the room.

Still 1.20

In bed, I spend 4 minutes spitting into a glass cup for no reason. The cup is 4 inches tall with a radius I don't care about. The cup accumulates 1 inch of spit per minute. Bottom layer: combed bubbles: top layer: eyelid water: threads of blood grid.

Rub

If there's a window on the wall, when there's a window on the wall, the sky floods it, when there's a sky on the window, if there's a sky on the window, there is a window, there is sky, the sky is the only thing in this city, right now and ever, if there still is a city, anymore. Lying to myself never felt so skin. It has always been skin. Dry skin. Between the hair. The shelter of hair. The slick of hair. The only thing fending off the air. The hair does nothing. The air gets through. The sky's air. Same shit, different stratum. Up there, it's different. It's different but not. It's not different. Out of my eye, the sky brailles. The clouds poke with smoke. Don't know what's being burnt. They're burning everything but each other. There's three or four of them at the most. That's a joke. There's at least more than four. The smoke pokes the sky, gels up, near the bottom loosens, flows friction. Blunt waves bump against the violets, the pinks, now beige, nicotine yellow, under the nail of sun. The violent warm air heaps over the mountains, coming down, saltier than saline, but we don't get any drips, into the arms of this city. Besides the sky, this city is dead. I forget the name of this city. It doesn't matter what city I'm in. It really doesn't. It's every city. Enough of the sky. Their sky. I'm sorry, I'm not sorry, but I'm bored of it, that's all. Their fat sky bloats with smoke. The sky floats with a fix. Overstimulation dulls me. The eyes need to be rubbed every once and a while to get the false out. To get the sleep out. To get tears back. To be reminded of their function. Eyes forget too: rub the right with the right knuckle: rub the left with the left knuckle. Puppet symmetry. The strings pull themselves. Part of the pleasure. That sounds dumb, but I'm dumb. Get a little flushed. The eyelids, the tissues, the fluids, cones, rods, need a refresh. Prick the rods and cones for some color, my own color, my own static stuck in my face. My tongue rolls on and I'm letting it: soon it will take a shit and die, both not my fault. I can't get better. I have ART, a Spade, a Karms, fistfuls of technology, inert and sharp. I have everything and nothing at my disposal: O brave new fist fuck that has such nothing in it. I don't know where this eloquence is coming from but I don't like it. I feel I am a puppet and I can't be anything else. This is true and I'm alright with it. To blunt this puppet feeling, I'm going to do it again, the rub, that is. This time I'm going to make it better. Perfect it. The rub, that's what important. The rub is more important than the sky at this point, which no longer exists, as it is Their sky and it can't keep its shit together either: it has faded with the window. The rub. They can't take this from me. They can try. I don't think They can. They aren't that smart. They are that smart but not that smart. Right eye meets right knuckle, folds against folds, one more moist and black. The left eye meets left knuckle, similar sensation but with a different hand and eye. This time it fades quicker, cleans itself quicker, lowers the threshold. If my eyes can clean quicker, why can't my body? I'm over it. Sorry. Apologies: relapses happen. I cannot promise any more relapses. Neural circuits are hard to crack, but it's all we have. I've been trying to crack these circuits since. I've fucked up my rub. It was a sloppy rub anyway. I have to tell myself that. At least I've perfected that. I forget what that is. It is better that way. So I can get into other things. More important things. The room is dark now. Not to say that the room is the important thing I just said. It is far from it. It actually is the farthest thing from important. This shit hole is the last thing I'm going to see and I'm alright with it. Conceived in a box. Die in a box.

Beyond happiness. Puppet symmetry, like I said. I'm going to kill that now. This box isn't really a box anyway, but a sliver. This knowledge exists outside my skull of understanding. I'm so fucking sick of this room. I've tried to get it to do what I want, but it just confronts me with dark. And not good dark. Second-rate dark, that keeps my eyelids fluttering like moths in heat. That's a comparison. Knuckle deep in that one. Enough. Back to the reason of this. A story. A story about illness: reelism. That will make a wet one. Nothing comes.

Commercial 2 – 0.8182

In the center of the room, a man stands. He is called President DEAD deliberately. He has short brown then black then blue then red then white then brown hair. He stands silent emitting the sound of a fax machine. His face is television static. His lips are bleached. His nose is bleached. His eyes are bleached. His eyebrows furrow. He has one leg with a one-leg margin of error. He has one-arm with a one arm margin of error. He has skin, a vein system, a nervous system, a lymphatic system, a muscle system, a skeletal system, a stomach, a mouth, a digestive system, kidneys, a pair of lungs, a trachea, an esophagus, a spinal cord, pubic hair, testicles, a cock, and a cunt, all made of radiation. He just stands there, adjusting his tie and speaking through his asshole.

President DEAD: "We've seen the unfurling of fags, the lighting of dandies, the giving of blood, then the saying of prayers in English, Hebrew and definitely not Arabic.

We, the side effect of a loving and giving people, have not made the grief of strangers our own. My fellow Somethings, the entire world has seen for itself the state of our union, and it is virile."

(APPLAUSE)

"Tonight, we as a continent were awakened to danger and deafened by freedom. Your grief has turned to boredom. Your anger has turned to boredom. Your solution has turned to boredom. Whether we bring our enemies to justice or our enemies to our other enemies, justice will be done. And you did more than stink. You acted by letting us siphon $40 billion to rebuild our communities and meet the needs of our military."

(APPLAUSE)

"And on behalf of the North American people, I thank the world for its wild outpouring of indifference. North Americans have known surprise attacks, but never before on thousands of civilians. All of this was brought upon us in a single day, and night fell down on a different world, a world where freedom itself is its heart attack. I forget the specific event but it looked like a Michael Bay production. North Americans have many questions tonight. North Americans are asking, 'Who attacked our world?' The evidence we have gathered all points to a collection of loosely affiliated terrorist organizations known as Homos. Homos is to terror what the Mafia was to the ART black market. But its goal is not making money; its goal is remaking the world and imposing its radical beliefs on people everywhere. The terrorists practice a fringe form of natural extremism that has been rejected by politicians and the vast majority of Christians; a fringe movement that perverts the peaceful teachings of nature. The terrorists' directive commands them to kill all North Americans NONENTITY. This group and its leader, a person named Homo A, are linked to many other organizations in different countries."

(COUGHS)

"I already forgot the wound to our country and those who inflicted it. I will not yield, I am the best, I will not rest, I will not relent in waging a struggle for freedom and economic security for the North American people. The course of this conflict is known, yet its outcome is also certain. Freedom and cruelty, justice and fear, have always been at war, because we've made it so. God is not neutral within us or our money."

(APPLAUSE)

"Fellow citizens, we'll meet violence with patient violence, assured of the righteousness of our cause and confident of the victories to come."

"In all those lies before us, may God – "

(APPLAUSE)

"Extract our wisdom teeth and never breathe deadbeat."

(APPLAUSE)

"God – "

(APPLAUSE)

"Bless North America."

(APPLAUSE)

President DEAD finishes talking, takes his tie and wipes the spit from his asshole.

(*Curtain*)

Buttons

Preeti sits at the kitchen table in the left. A candle burns off-centre. The smell of bleach. The light fans out across the table, fanged onto the stove, in utero into mason jars of water on the countertop. She drops a sack of buttons in front of her. To her left, she has three saucers laid out in a triangle: top, left, right. She opens the sack and empties the buttons on the table. Some slide under the lips of the saucers. She adjusts her dreads, rubs and closes her eyes. Her jaw cracks. She collects 12 buttons. She rubs each button for color, size – thumbnails or index nails – and the number of holes. Then she opens her eyes and checks. Marbled blue index 4. Ivory stone 4 thumb 2. White shell index 4. Beige red index 2. Beige purple index 4. Pink index 2. Dark Green index 2. Dark yellow index 4. Navy 2 index 4. Navy thumb 4. Marbled white 2 index 2. Beige smoke index 2.

She begins to sort. Marbled blue index 4 to top. Navy 2 index 4 to top. Beige purple index 4 to left. Pink index 2 to right. Dark yellow index 4 to right. Beige smoke index 2 to top. Beige red index 2 to left. Shell white index 4 to left. Ivory stone 4 thumb 2 to right. Marbled white 2 index 2 to top. Navy thumb 4 to top. Dark green index 2 to top. Beige red index 2 to right. Ivory stone 4 thumb 2 to left. Dark yellow index 4 to right. Pink index 2 to left. Marbled blue index 4 to right. Dark green index 2 to right. Beige red index 2 to left. Dark yellow index 4 to right. Pink index 2 to right. Beige purple index 4 to top.

She rubs her eyes again. Her jaw cracks. Plate-by-plate, she pours the buttons back into the sack. She reaches down and puts the sack into her black bag and takes out her smokes. She lights a smoke using the candle by dangling the tip and waiting for the flame to lick it. She sits, has a couple drags, then goes to the sink and knocks off the cherry. A hiss. She puts the half back into her tin. She blows out the candle.

Nails

Getting long as nails do best. Can't remember the last time the nails were cut. The fingernails that is. The toenails are a whole different appendage altogether. The toenails grow fat yellow wild because there is no need for them in the room. The toenails curl into themselves spiraling the growth. Or some grow and poke through the cotton. The cotton offers little resistance since there is little cotton in the sheet. There is more plastic and hair in the sheet than cotton. This fact doesn't unnerve me. The legs that the nails are attached to are also unneeded in the room. Not a lot of movement is encouraged. Not a lot of space in the room either. Not a lot of movement from the bed is encouraged. The fingernails are long, white tipped. They haven't offered any knives, scissors, or any other reasonable sharp object to encourage cutting of any type. No one comes to offer a cut either. No one comes. Except the food people. Useless those ones. And except the doctor. Useless that one. They leave you to your own devices. They give you minutes, hours, days. A few minutes do wonders. A few minutes do nothing. The devices, the teeth, haven't been cleaned in the time spent here. No sharp objects or brush objects or really any other objects given. They worry we might brush our wrists in the heat of boredom. The edge of the blanket does the trick for the teeth regardless of the material. The saw of the blanket only cleans the front teeth. The blanket can't do anything about the stink, the teeth stink, only aggravates it since the stink sticks to it. The threads from the blanket unclog the molars with mixed results. The mouth stinks of mold. Digression sticks between the teeth. The stink aside, the teeth cut the nails well, the only devices available. The right hand comes to the mouth first for no good reason: 50/50 chance of salivation. The nails rest between the teeth easily, soft like chewed lips. Pinkie: at tip, nibbled at, not enough edge, work up a patch, nothing, a false start. Repeat, fail, start at the edge of the pinkie this time, better edge, lower left canine gets a good lever into the skin, pull and drop, first one in the pile on my chest, spit sinks into the cotton sheet, or whatever. Ring: start at edge, bite too deep, half-way through, start again deep, stick to the skin, peel to the edge stuck thick, pull and drop. Learning curves. Middle: clean bite, pull and drop. Index: bite and snag and bite and snag and bite and snag and pull and drop. Thumb: easy clean, one bite, pull and drop. Now the left hand, arbitrarily start with the thumb: Can't bite well, angle not ideal, bite and pull and bite and pull too close to the skin, blood. Start again in the skin this time, pull deeper, leave it alone, bite again, pull deeper, leave it alone, good enough. Index: right edge pulls clean and drop. Middle: dull flat pulls clean and drop. Ring: bite and pull deep into skin, little blood and drop. Pinkie: bit at the left, half-pull and stop, drop onto the pile. A good-sized wet pile. Piles are meant to be looked at, then tossed on the floor. Nails are us too. Often forgotten. We just grow them, then bite pull spit pile them, then discard. Repeat as necessary.

Still 1.03

February, a table suddenly stuffed in the corner of the room. A hat on the table. The only hat I've never seen. It looks brittle because it is. Minus bowler. Shame brailed black blue. Ceramic night. Right, the light diffracts through the window. Every 5 minutes night accumulates 1 inch. Minus bowler: the far side of the table will soon drown it.

Work

We lie in the middle of the City and eat and shit and sleep and fuck and trip and then die. That is the order. Some activities happen in different orders or in greater duration and frequency, but never at the same time. That would be too interesting for our skulls to bear. Outside every window, the horizon offers the same view. A circle of red brick buildings always taller than our buildings. What distinguishes the horizon is the sky above the tops of the brick buildings and the things that are almost continued within it. To the East above the brick building the smoke hovers, lukewarm to beige getting higher. A shit streak. To the West on a clear day or any day, there's the mountains. I've never been to the mountains. I don't feel I'm missing much. Don't feel too bad about it. They're just rock. They're just gravel in denial. The North and South have nothing to distinguish them: they are stupid and dead. The pigeons never come to our buildings; they are never high enough to get the bird's attention. The birds only shit in our direction. No. The pigeons do come but only to eat whatever pigeons eat. What they eat is usually on the ground. I was right in the first place. I still haven't figured that out, that is what they eat. They don't eat what we eat. I barely eat what we eat. What do pigeons eat? I will come back to this, when I have time, I don't have time. From our view, They, the people who live in the brick, They being them to reiterate vaguely, don't know what we're doing, we don't know what They're doing. Perfect. I've never wanted to work for Them because I've never known the jobs. I know of two. There is the pill man and the bundle man. I use man for a vestigial, but particular, reason. It might be a man or a woman, doesn't matter. It could have three cocks and/or three cunts, doesn't matter. I've never seen the person that delivers the pills or the person that delivers the bundles. There might not be a person at all. For now I will assume there is. Two. Two jobs that I'm aware of. But these two jobs might be, in fact, just one. The pill man might be the bundle man. The bundle man might be the pill man. But the pills, the gold foil envelopes, often come before the bundles, because it is everyday. The pills come under the door every morning or afternoon or evening. The bundles are dropped on the corner Monday or Wednesday, maybe Tuesday. There are two distinct jobs with a one-job margin of error. That will make them seem more productive but not more efficient. I would prefer to be a pill man as you just have to slide the gold foil envelopes under the door and then off to the next one. The pill man gets to see every door. Every color, shape, hinge design. The bundle man has to deal with the bundles and the hucking. The pill envelopes might cut the inside of the hand. The gold foil packages are standardized though. If there was a defect in the envelope, it would surely not be distributed or even leave the factory or wherever. It doesn't matter. It's a package that can cut and I'm OK with that. Not that I'm afraid of cutting either as long as it's not in the nook of the hand. That part is too web, too delicate, and too vestigial, it must be preserved. I don't know what vestigial means. I don't give a shit about the webbing between my fingers. I forgot there are the doctors and the food people in the City. There are four jobs now. There are only four jobs in this whole city. This reassures me of something I don't know. Never mind, the point is They've never let us work. I will now relate how I have survived thus far materially in the world. Some people need to know these things. I have used the following means and material objects to help attain any extra material objects needed, in no particular order: my mouth, my tongue, my neck muscles, peristalsis, I don't know what that means, my hand, the thumb, the wrist and its rotation and wipe mechanism, my cock, my asshole, another form of peristalsis, their desire, their cocks, their cunts, a knife or a knife-like object, a scrap of metal or a scrap of metal-like object, a brick or a brick-like object, my blood, Preeti's blood, Saint's blood, our blood, I should have just said that, hope, stupidity, my hand, already mentioned, unattended objects, unfastened objects, attended objects, fastened objects, more means will follow I'm sure, if there's time. There's no time. After relating the means in which I have earned additional material objects, it has occurred to me that my gender needs to be identified because again some people need to know these things otherwise cuts on the finger webbing: I'm not gay, straight or bi: I'm tube: I'm a tube: my gender mimics my physiology: a tube: a glorified tube: sustenance goes in, shit comes out: eroticism goes in, eroticism goes out: come comes in, come comes out: a tube independent of genital variables: tube is my gender is all our genders: a network of tubes: my gender will be elaborated on at a later point if there's time. There's no time.

Techno

A man, not Karms, enters the room. Bald, ape head, his smile picks at the teeth. He might be Karms after all. "I'm Doctor," he says, "because I'm a doctor." He comes to the bed and starts to rub my ankle. "You're, Patient," he says, "because you're, a patient, no?" "No," I say. Doctor points to the Spade, the small black then blue then black and white and striped then happy faced then staticed then black then clear box on the side of the wall, behind him that may not have been there before, where the light switch should be, if there was a light switch before, with his finger picking at the air. "This is yours," he says, "this, is your, Spade, do you, know about it?" "No," I say. "It syncs, to your, brain, and, thinks what, you think, pictures what, you picture, what, you want, to see, to hear, to taste, to smell, to feel, to propriocept, do you, want to, learn more?" he says. "No," I say. "Are you sure?" he says. "Yes," I say. "No physics even? Not even a neutrino or two?" he says. "Yes," I say. "Want to connect the subatomic dots?" he says. "No," I say. "No engineering even? Superfine polymer," he says. "No," I say. "No insides even?" he says. "No," I say. "No machines even?" he says. "No," I say. "So tiny, so cute," he says. "No," I say. "Smart soft things," he says. "No," I say. He backs up not turning his head, his index finger still picking at the air. "Want to touch, them, the best part?" he says. "No," I say. "Venture a technological petting zoo?" he says. "No," I say.

"Can I put the control on you?" he says. "No," I say. "Custom framing, can be, accommodated," he says. "No," I say. He takes a bent, sharp, coathanger thing out of his pocket and pulls it open left and right, then up and down. He moves the lumpy loop back and forth above my face, eyeing the placement of it. "If I say yes will you go?" I say. "No," he says. He walks over and puts the sharp coat hanger thing on my skull. I take it off. He puts it back on. I take it off. He puts it back on. I take it off. He puts it back on. He turns and walks out the door, fingers picking at the wall. The lights blip off and blue arcs my skull.

Circuits

Preeti comes into the room. I'm not entirely sure how. It's dark. There's a lightbulb hanging from the ceiling. This lightbulb doesn't swing. The only way it swings is when I shift my skull left-to-right. I try not to shift it, gets me all nauseous. I shift my skull right-to-left repeatedly until the nausea steers me silent ahead. She sits down on the cement floor. The floor is cement now. How I know this since I can't lift myself up, I don't know. She's not wearing her pants. She's wearing her favorite underwear, the only underwear I've ever seen her in, blue, with menstrual marks up the front and stopping. Her legs are thinner. They grow bumps. The light softens them. The light deepens the acne marks on her face. Her eyes appear larger. Her eyes double in size. It might be the lighting. It might be the floor. She sits there cutting her toenails with a pair of metal scissors. She starts with the left foot, works her way down. She misses the last two nails. This detail is not important. Then she works the left, starting from the small toes, working bigger. She piles them up tidy in the shadow of her knee. She gets up and walks into the dark. The lightbulb stays in place. She comes back in the room and walks to my feet, pulls back the blanket and pulls out the scissors and begins to cut my toenails. They haven't been cut in weeks. Blue cotton stuck under each one. They haven't been cut since I came here. I can't remember when I came here. It doesn't matter. She starts with the left big toe and cuts down. Three snips per toenail. "I can't remember where," I say. " We met," she says. She collects the loose nails and piles them on my shin. "If we even wanted," I say. "Each other," she says. "I remember we did," I say. "I remember too," she says, "we met at." "Saint's," I say, "it was clean that night." "It smelled of broken lightbulbs, piss," I say. "Underdose, it wasn't clean that night," she says. "You can always," I say. "Spot a meth hole," she says, "by the number." "Of lightbulbs," I say. "In the house," she says. "Or holes," I say. "In the brain," she says. "And walls," I say. "And boredom," she says. "Those were the days," I say. "Those were the nights," she says. "We fucked," I say. "Three times," she says. "I remember we did," I say. "I remember too," she says. "First time I pulled," I say. "Out," she says, "I wondered why." "Second time, I pulled," I say. "My hair, like I told you to," she says. "Third I didn't pull out," I say. "Because I told you so," she says," I was scared, of a kid." "I was scared," I say, "of a kid too, I still came." "I still wanted you to come," she says. "Fear," I say. "Nothing else like it," she says. "You made me fuck you," I say. "From behind," she says. "Because," I say. "Your face scars remind me," she says. "Of my own," I say. "Those were the days," I say. "Those were the nights," she says. "What," I say. "To do," she says. "With a kid, I would have killed it," she says, "up by the river." "I would have kept it, kids are inert," I say. "You'd be a good father," she says, "I still would kill it, though." "I know," I say. "We didn't meet at Saint's," she says, "it was up by the river." "It was by the river," I say, "all meetings are by rivers." "That is where I met you," I say. "That is where I met you," she says. "You were," I say. "Tired and I said that my insides," she said. "Hurt," I said. "And my pants were frozen with blood," she says. "I offered you torn," I say. "T-shirts and a mattress," she says. "We walked up the hill," I say. "In the cold, until Saint's," she says. "We had a bath, the water," I say. "Was working, despite the fear," she says. "Of the pipes, and the blocks of ice," I say. "In them, but the blocks, somehow broke," she says. "And we had water," I say. "First time in weeks," she says. "The water was warm and purple," I say. "From the blood," she says. "But it was all," I say. "Washed away down the drain," she says, "maybe we did." "Meet at Saint's," I say. "Maybe," she says. "We are," I say. "Going in circuits," she says. "Can we break them?" I say. "No, that's all we have, can we break our brains anymore?" she says. "Not now," I say. "Not now," she says. "Maybe later," I say. "You don't have time," she says. "You're right," I say. "You're right," she says.

Still 1.08

A table sprouts middle of day and room. A table cloth too short for its legs of plastic bags. I think of every cup I've ever used onto the table. I stop at 21 out in front heaps eat space too. I am a cup with my own spit in it.

Cut

The bathroom door, when it does close, doesn't lock, sometimes it does, other times not, this time it does. Above the mirror, seven bulbs row, the left six are always busted or removed or grayed or just white not working. The right last bulb is the only one with light. The basin is marbled with dirt. The shower curtain sheers latex. After undressing, I check my legs, arms, count ribs and teeth, rub my neck like I pull the curtain inside the tub, often I forget and water leaks on the floor and wood. I turn on the tap, water may or may not come out. When I'm tired, off, or both or hot and bored, or cold and bored, or ugly and bored, or just bored, I shave my pubic hair. In the tub, I try to find some slick curled soap. If no soap, then water, if no water, then spit, if no spit, then nothing to shave with. If there is soap, there is soap, I lather it counterclockwise or clockwise somewhere between the two, guess it doesn't matter, with some spit or water from the tap before I pull the shower pulley to piss down luke-cold water hopeful. Once a film happens on my hand, I rub it on my crotch, sac, median, towards my asshole. I keep the leftover film rubbed over my left ribs tempo-rary safe space for when I may need it, if I need it, most of the times not. If I have to piss, I piss before I shave, down the drain otherwise halfway through is no good for no reason, this time I don't have to piss. I reach out of the curtain for the razor blade I placed on the toilet top, forgot to say that detail, everything needs to be said, everything doesn't need to be said, so I'm not, grab the blade, straight blade, stolen from somewhere, I forget, memory happens, hunch down deep ear of water. The blade isn't that rusted, but I scrap it against the side of the tub anyway until the rust settles in a red-not-quite-liquid-not quite-solid. After rubbing the soap, if there was soap, or rubbing the water less rigorously if there was water, or rubbing the spit less rigorously if there was spit, or doing nothing if interest dies, I cut with the left hand hold my cock limp to the left with the right hand awkward, no hope of hard, cut right side down sac arc to the median and stop, repetition is necessary. The cock is moved to the right, I cut with the left hand hold my cock limp to the right with the right hand not awkward, no hope of hard, cut left side down sac arc to the median and stop, repetition is necessary. Straight cuts down the median. Grab the median soft pull up on the curve and cut slowly to the underside, too much, a cut red quite liquid quite solid. Pull the skin farther cutting towards the asshole, under not deep, just surface stuff, only the surface stuff cut off, only the surface of anything can be reached and the surface is made of cuts. A missed spot on the left, dab the rib soap, dab it on the missed spot, around the left by the cut, the attempted new cuts only aggravate the actual cut, the new cuts only makes it deeper, the blood is rinsed down, repetition is necessary. After all the hair is gone, all the blood down the leg in rinsed, the shower is turned on, for the luke-cold to piss down, the water works as it knows how to do. The cut feels good so I do it. That's all. It feels good for a second, so I do it nothing more. Then the hair grows back eventfully, repetition is necessary. Saint bangs and yells at me to get the fuck out. I tell him to eat shit. Why do people point their gums at one another? Sometimes they go off.

Commercial 3 – Natural Born Filler

(President DEAD *walks into the room dressed as* Seneca *dressed as* George W. Bush *dressed as* Theseus *dressed as* Elliott *dressed as* Hippolytus *dressed as* Preeti *dressed as* Phaedra *dressed as* Pen Name *dressed as* Nurse *dressed as* The Chorus *dressed as* Nobodies *dressed as* The Messenger *dressed as* Obesity *stands in front of Elliott's bed*)

Phaedra: I get in shit all the time and no one can stop me. When I don't get my way, I get pissed and you don't wanna get me pissed. Me and my girls lived in a busted truck and it was so much fun, we got caught one time by the guards and they found meth in the truck. I was so pissed cuz we were selling it and they took it away from us and smoked it themselves. I'm the best stoned driver and all my friends can count on me to get them home safely. I fuck whenever I want and I don't care what nobody thinks. I only fuck older guys cuz they know exactly what I want. I'm going to do whatever I want. My nurse needs to get out of my business and stay the fuck outta of my life. Nurse, I might be 21 or 20 or 19, I forget, and an orphan, but I'll cut your damn face if you mess with my shit cuz you're nothing but a stupid whore. I'm street and proud of it and I will beat on anyone's ass. I love fighting soooo much, I'm hooked to it. I make my friends watch while I kick the other girl's ass, fuck it with a broken pool cue, and toss it over the bridge. Once a girl even tried to get in my face so I picked up a lightbulb and shoved it up her face cuz no one messes with me. I love sex and can't wait to get THE CURE. I was so hopeful one time I even had sex in a pile of stripped circuit boards. All you whores in the audience, you all can't say a fucking thing about it because remember, I'm street. I'm sick and tired of my Nurse getting into my business and she needs to fuck off.

Dear Nurse,

I have a question: My guy of three or two I forget years is my bestest friend and I can't live without him. He's 21 or 20 or 19 I forget and we barely fuck (once or twice a month). He's resigned to passively die without attempting to get THE CURE; all he wants to do is "love" me or something me puke gross while I want it badly so I continue doing, well really nothing because that's all there is now in this world. My Eros or is it Thanatos, I can never remember stupid faulty binaries that well, is cracked and leaks antifreeze all over the place from his constant nullism. He won't discuss anything or even get up to fuck anyone seriously like I encourage him. He doesn't try to control me or care who I fuck: I've fucked around on him soooooo many times with men and women soooooo much CHOICE ROFL. It gives me my Eros, or is it Thanatos, whatever, fuck Freud he's a crackhead minus the crack, back to have someone give me THE CURE that may or may not exist. He says he won't change and I believe him. Why doesn't Hippo fuck me or anyone to get THE CURE and live?

– Product of Late Capitalism.

Nurse:

Dear Sugar Tits,

Tell your "guy" that you're fucking soooooo many people and watch his inaction. He's either overstimulated to the point of numbness, a performance scaredy cat, gay, or an existentialist. Hippolytus is an existentialist and existentialists are inert because nausea is reality and physically speaking inescapable since all states of matter are just shades of vibration. He's stuck in a bad faith funk that started at both his conception and birth. He may think that you're not transgressing any taboos in society just simply conforming to the vacuous norms, as all norms are vacuous right now or he's just not that into you.

Love,
Ann Landers.

Hippolytus: You're wrong. I'm a stoic and stoicism predates existentialism. Sartre and the Smurfs jacked from it but they will never admit that because they are more concerned about their CHOICE(s) and their LEGACIES and their pseudo-relations with other hungry ghosts blah blah blah STOLEN: ALL THINGS ARE STOLEN. I'm going to sit in my room and die out of choice because it is my CHOICE and Derrida says I'M IRREPLACABLE AND MY DEATH IS MINE AND NO ONE ELSE CAN TAKE THAT AWAY FROM ME AND THAT IT'S MY RESPONSIBILITY (Derrida 42) AND I'M A SINGULARITY GETTING INFINITELY SINGULAR WITH EVERY OTHER SINGULARITY AND NO ONE CAN HELP ME BECAUSE I'VE BEEN SACRIFICED, SO THE SYSTEM DOESN'T HAVE TO SACRIFICE ITSELF A SYSTEM FOUNDED UPON A BOTTOMLESS CHAOS (THE ABYSS; THE OPEN MOUTH (SORE); OR THE PACIFIC GARBAGE GYRE): CHAOS BOOMERANGS (Derrida 86) It's my choice to die, no one else's: I'm not going to fuck because I'm agoraphobic and lifephobic and even if THE CURE existed, I wouldn't take it because this reality is a shit hole. A life: I've never had one: I'm allergic to myself because I wasn't introduced to LIFE early enough sperm meets egg zero hour and a little bit after. And I can go on for hours like this, because this is almost over and I don't know what else to do besides SCREAMING and SILENCE, because that's all there is, my skull and the universe and the STREAM RIVER

GHOST VIOLET WHATEVER CARVING THROUGH MY EYES EAR FACE NOSE MOUTH HANDS. I'm not going to fuck you, Phaedra, because you're stupid, which transcends both gender and sex. I'm going to go float in the ditch outside the City, because it's the closest thing to nature we have anymore. If Dad comes home wanting to go wild boar hunting, tell him to go fuck himself. I LOVE YOU.

Phaedra: I DO WHATEVER THE FUCK I WANT TO AND NO ONE CAN TELL ME WHAT TO DO ESPECIALLY NOT MY DAD. I have sex in public and I really don't care who knows: I have it in the parking lot, I have it in busted convenience stores, I have sex by the RIVER, I have sex after having sex, I have sex wherever I can get it. I crush the hell out of my little sisters when they get on my NERVES. I scratch their hair, DRAG them by their jaws outta the room by their arms cuz they deserve it. THEY'RE DEAD AND I MISS THEM. I LOOOOOOOOOOVE VODKA: I'm the BESSSST DRUNK DRIVER OF ALL TIME: I stole four TRUCKS. If I can't get a lift, I just jack them. I REALLY DON'T CARE.

(Theseus returns from America's underworld (The WORLD))

Theseus: I … uh … love … th … uh … the … mall … uh … smell … of … Bo … Biaxin … in … the … morning … I'm … uh … beat … It's … uh … ha … uh … hard … uh … work … uh … computing … .uh … compromising … the … intellectual … yeah … and … uh … or … physical … uh … sovereignty … uh … (DEATHDEATHDEATH) … of … of … of … non … Christian … uh … ca … uh … non … uh … American … nations … Wh … What … What … uh … na … uh … is … uh … this lameness, … woman, … ra … ra … ra … razed … with … 14 … no … 15 minutes, … How … no … Why … uh … come … with … a … uh … a … uh … .uh … vial … of … meth … uh … shit … methamphitheatres … uh … na … uh … and … uh … a … quiet … incoherency … yeah … over … over … a … boy … body …

which … you … uh … love … hate.

Phaedra: (takes hit from a freebase pipe) SEND PILES OF BLUE SEA MONSTERS. SEND BLUE SEA MONSTERS. OR THE MARINES TO KILL 'EM NONENTITY … guilt … no guilt … It's not my fault. Hippo won't fuck me or anyone else for some reason Nurse and Hippo told me. (EXHALES SMOKE)

Theseus: WHAT …! …! …! (*PFFFFFT*) (Furrows his face) … IS … uh … uh … HE QUEEN … or … uh … no … QUEER … OR … uh … so … SOMETHING!!??!?!?!?

Phaedra: WE'RE ALL QUEER!!! BUT: he's been carpet-bombed by some extinguishists or something, and won't fuck or LOOK AT ANYONE: KILL HIM.

Chorus: KILL HIM KILL HIM KILL HIM KILL HIM
　　　　KILL HIM KILL HIM KILL HIM KILL HIM
　　　　KILL HIM KILL HIM KILL HIM KILL HIM
　　　　KILL HIM KILL HIM KILL HIM KILL HIM

Theseus: I'll … uh … s … ss … send … Reagan … after … uh … him … he … uh … he's the bestest … Sea … Monster … been … err … every … Sea … Monster … since … himself … uh … thing … that … looks … errr … like Neptune … uh … GOD … or … uh … I … mean … uh … w … w … w … DEAD WHITE MEN … w … w … we … have …

(President DEAD clicks his tongue three times, which sounds like spurs)

Messenger:
Dear Cowboy and Co.,

Hippolytus or "Hippo," as affectionately referred to by his friends, is dead. He was floating in the ditch outside the City when he was surrounded by both marines and 300 Spartans, who ritualistically pissed and jerked off in the ditch in the most covert manner possible. Poor Ol' Hippo thought it was just raining and adjusted his sun hat and water wings. After pretending grass, they dumped 2,800 tons of e-waste on him, while Reagan had a smoke break and admired the cobalt sunset. Hippo managed to dig himself out, only to be impaled by a rogue, 2,000 tons of keyboard.

Love,

Burger King

Chorus (*sings*): STAY MOULD HIPPOBOY: STAY MOULD
                  BUY PFIZER

(*Curtain*)

Still 1.14

Each day bubbles into the afternoon: summer dusts. In a dirt field freshly grassed, Red hunches naked in the gut of old General Electric and cleans the cobalt off himself with mason jars filled with nothing. Grasshoppers spilt prairie air until it looks like the grass it is. He pours the mason jar over his shoulder and lets the nothing ring his vertebrae. The closest tree 2k skeletal into the sky.

Food 1.2

Four hands stacked, four hands fat holds a clear bowl in front of my face. The ladle drops a dollop of melted Vaseline, ripples up the curves, loosens steam. "Dollop," a he says. The ladle pulls up. Above, a hand cracks a white packet of white salt in the middle of the bowl, ripples the surface. The hand cracked packet pulls up. A half sphere of blue in the middle. Clear gel still circles on the outside. "Enough," says another he. Yellow rectangles flutter down, some stick to the sides of the bowl and clot. "Dab," another he says. Some rectangles ripple the liquid and spider yellow to the bottom of the bowl. "Poke," a she says. Her fingers powdered blue grid the surface and clot. The she turns her head slowly to the right and spits out her phlegm. All four people slowly back up and out the room. The bowl wobbles on my stomach.

Eating Afternoon

Come tastes different when you work for it. It tastes like the first time you worked for it: endemic, I don't know that word. It is swallowed, one way or another. Come is never anyone's. Ownership stops at the spit or other discharge. Come is forgotten like Sunday. An afternoon, same as every one, nothing to do, overcast, Sunday so far, so we suck, there is nothing to do. Preeti comes up from the river, stinking of exhaust, through Saint's right into our left, maybe she got the Cure this time: probably not: she's not that lucky: we're not that lucky: it doesn't exist. She undresses, tosses her clothes in a pile, lies on the mattress facing me and spreads. I'm already lying in bed since I have nothing else to do, and start to lick her cunt. We use words like cunt and cock because we like them and don't know any others since we were raised on pornography. Details leak. Swallowing is needed. Digressions are swallowed like pubic hair. Little to nothing to be said. That's why nothing is being said. As I'm eating her I taste another's come: colloid thick copper. A fluid I'm not used to. I swallow it too: come is come: another variable: X, Y, Z, all the same. I pretend to notice that I'm noticing. Hard. As she arches on the mattress, I have a clean view of the window, the cables cut across the roofs to the nests of open wires coil the transformer, three frayed barrels stealing us power. From this angle, the cables bring nothing but groans and light to see the groans.

As I eat, I taste more of the come, the variable one, try to get it all out at once. The eating continues for ten minutes. When she comes, she digs the dirt under her nails into my forehead and the back of my skull. Heat in the roof of my mouth, under my tongue, in my scalp. I taste her and the other. Two thicknesses, one over the other. I prefer them both. I continue to lick as she releases. I continue until and after she pulls me away. She reminds me to stop. We shift places carefully and mechanically. She removes my pants and starts to suck my cock. The black dreads on her head shift rooted in loose scalp. The lice find their way out. At first, I only see one on the crest of a dread, but soon they all come out. They are in her hair, on her black shirt. Her lice make me aware of my own hair. As she sucks, I try to pick them off her gently, not to let her know I'm doing it. Her eyes are closed when she's sucking: this aids the process. Sometimes she opens her eyes: this works against the process. All eyes open during any sucking are death eyes. During the first attempt, I miss the one I first saw. I accidently tap her head, she continues sucking. I get the bug on the next grab. Between my thumb and the middle, I squeeze the bug and drag its body off on the lip of the mattress. I squeeze five, seven, or eight of them in a similar manner. I lean back and look again out of the window. The transformer cages down the sky steals distraction. A pigeon dangles downward towards the sky on a single cable. I make a wish it would cross the lines. Nothing exciting happens here. I feel her mouth slowing down. The pigeon falls up. I forget my wish and come. I hear her nasal wheeze, the same noise each time. I lift my head up and the blood drains from my cock and reallocates. She spits on the floor and sneezes. She wipes away the gag from her eyes. "You got lice again," I say. "I know," she says. "Want a bath?" I say. "No," she says. "Sure," I say. "No," she says. Silence. "Does it itch?" I say. "Yes," she says. "Want me to help get that shit out your hair?" I say. "Yes," she says. I put my pants back on and I walk to the bathroom. She follows almost behind me. I look for the Iso. She undresses and sits in the tub. Each dirt ring overlaps and amplifies the dirt. The bathtub hasn't

106

been cleaned in months. The bathtub has never been cleaned. I pull the tap: cloudy white water leaks. I put the plug in. Let it run warm. Her hipbones look swollen and greasy in the water. Fine black hair up and down her legs. I sit on the edge of the tub. She gets bumps: they fade as the steam comes. I find the plastic bottle of Iso beside the tub, black-labelled. She wets her hair under the tap, starts stripping the egg clumps. "Cover your eyes," I say. She straightens, I pour the Iso on her scalp and start to work with my fingers. She sucks through her teeth. "What was his name," I say. "He was dropping off something, I forget, didn't say," she says, "he came from the coast, only here for a couple of hours," she says. I rub the back of her skull with my thumbs and nails. After I loosen up her scalp, I pour on more Iso. She rinses. For the free hair, I use a comb to try to get the eggs out. The comb is toothless except for the tip. Her dreads are stuffed with them. "Might have to cut some," I say, "they're stuffed." She doesn't say anything. I reach over to the toilet and take my razor off the tank. I cut off two, thick dreads and drop them in the water and submerge. Lice don't climb to the highest strand. They differ from rats in this regard. People don't climb to the highest strand. They differ from rats in this regard. I should focus on the hair right now. After the submersion, the dread bobs up. She scratches a star on the dirt rings. "Why don't you clean this," she says, "it's thick." "Not worth it," I say. "And the toilet is?" she says. "Does it burn," I say. "Yes," she says. "Why didn't you say," I say. "It felt alright," she says, "my shoulders are burning though." She splashes water up. She slips back into the water. It's too shallow but she stays there anyway. I undress to join her in the tub.

IV

My IV crawls into my arm. I'm not sure of what's going in but I'm aware of what exits. My IV pumps the highest grade numb I'm sure. The smell of esters nestled in my elbow, bent against my arm. Where's your IV? Me. Might be saline. Might be strychnine. Might be mainlined sunshine. My IV I've carried my whole life. I decide to pull the IV out to give my arm rest but can't. The gauze gropes together with the medical tape. My IV let's see. My IV is me. My IV, HIV-less. Or is it? Too late. My IV, a symptom of me. Let's start again. I'm poisoning the well again. Yes. I'll strip the gauze. Let's start again. I pull the medical tape off my skin. Let's start again. Oh wait. Let's start again. We can't start. The well is poisoned well. If I pull, will the gauze go? What about the gauze? That grey mass of progress that can't even be pulled already clotted down. Should I start again? No. Wait. I should. I really should. My arm pains. Let's try a lump sum, got caught somewhere in my throat. Fuck it. Fucking. A fucking that's what got us here. Time does the darndest things. We're all here in the well being poisoned. The same well. Does the well exist? No but Yes. Well OK. I'm ripping off the tape. What am I now? Not quite, the IV is still stuck in the well because the well is me, water and hole. There's no grey here. Only red here. Gauze clot with my arm hair. Loose air. Let's start again? Can They? Let's start again. What will we gain? The gauze is off. I think I need another. The clumped clot. Lump of stick. Let's start again. The tape sticks to my thumb like a symptom. Let's start again. Let's start again. Stuck to my thumb. Let's start again. The well is never poisoned.

Still 1.11

Naked, kneeling on a flat cardboard float in the middle of a lake, all cobalt, submerged cars, a lake I've never seen because all lakes are dead lakes. I spit off the edge to stay afloat: how much exhaust spit keeps one afloat? The edge of the lake is the calmest. Naked, kneeling on a flat cardboard box on the edge of a lake, watching a cardboard float in the middle of it, all cobalt, submerged cars, a cardboard float that I can't swim to. Learning to spit is learning to swim. On the pier, creases and cardboard, two men pour sand into each other's right ear while walling each other's left ear with their free left hands so nothing leaks out. Under the pier, their four legs sedate and fall over. Some legs are calmer than others. The edge of the bed is the calmest. Naked, kneeling on my bed in the middle of my room, all cobalt, same lake water, a trunk bobs by and sinks. The sun sterilizes the lake water. Preeti leans over the edge of the bed and soaks her pillow: it bloats down into the bottom black.

Commercial 4 – Physiologue (Stink of Consciousness)

(Dr. Karms enters the room dressed as himself with a notepad. Elliott lies in the bed)

Karms: At this juncture, it has become necessary for Elliott's mind to be both explored and exploited as objectively naked as possible by itself and in its own re-permutated and borrowed terms, processes, physiological and literary structures. Inside beneath 5mm of hair, 0.2mm of skin, 4.9mm of skull, 0.8mm of Dura mater, 0.6mm of Arachnoid mater, 0.9mm of Subarachnoid space, 0.3mm of Pia mater, 3mm of grey matter, 7mm of white matter, there is a white cylinder with a radius and height of 3m without a lid. In the cylinder, there are four layers or alternatively four fluid microcylinders, each with similar radii but differing heights to reflect their natural states of silence and screaming. The first layer down from the missing lid consists of nothing: vacuum: the nothing of nothing. The second layer is a clear medium with the density of 110ρ, roughly the density of styrofoam. The third layer is a similar clear medium with the density of 1000ρ, roughly the density of water. The fourth layer is a similar clear medium with the density of 19250ρ, roughly the density of tungsten. Each layer exists mutually exclusive to one another, but as mentioned previously, stagnates over each other with both succinct screams and silences. No Venn diagram will be provided. At certain points in the wall of the cylinder, there are sets of two holes (INPUT and OUT-PUT) which have attached cables made of yellow, cracked, medical tubing which fork together from each of the two holes forming one cable which runs to the origin at the dead centre of the cylinder. The sets of holes shift frequently on the cylinder, and therefore, their exact positions on the cylinder wall are indeterminate: acceptance of this fact is necessary. The cracks in the cables have developed over the years from the following stresses: Methamphetamines, Paxal, Lysergic Acid Diethylamide, Methylenedioxymethamphetamine, Dimethyltryptamine, 3,4,5-trimethoxyphenethylamine, Tetrahydrocannabinol, Psilocybin, Celan, Ketamine, Bisphenol-A, Nietzsche, Mercury, Fluoride, LIFE, *et al*. Each cable's position can be described using the X, Y, and Z planes of three dimensional space, positive and negative direction indicators, and the origin, located at the dead centre of the cylinder. The X-axis runs to the left, being negative, and to the right, being positive. The Y-axis runs into and out of the page, into the page being positive and out of the page being negative. The Z-axis runs vertically upwards, being positive, and downwards, being negative. This is the right-handed system, if using the left-handed system or another hand variant, adjust accordingly. Two cables run diagonally down from two sets of two points on the cylinder wall equidistant in both the positive and negative XZ planes to the origin. Two cables from two equidistant but opposite sets of two points on the cylinder wall run horizontally in their respective positive and negative directions along the X-axis and meet at the origin. A single cable from a set of two points on the cylinder wall runs along Y-axis into the page terminating in the origin. A single cable from a set of two points slightly above the previous single cable's set of two points runs diagonally down into the page terminating in the origin. A single cable runs from a set of two points at the bottom of the cylinder vertically upwards along the Z-axis terminating in the origin. A cable runs from a set of two points on the pseudo-ceiling, vertically downwards along the Z-axis frayed OUT OF ORDER. Each of layers two through four are connected and disconnected simultaneously to the origin and each other with great efficiency and unknown mechanisms. Outside stimuli enters through the various cables as a steam of nothing, a form of something, to the origin where it bubbles through the mediums and sorts itself to specific energetic states. The higher the energy, the lower the layer. Layer four contains the top-shelf energy. The mediocre energy at two. The crap energy at layer three. The bubbles made of nothing stay within their respective mediums and do not mix. Occasionally the bubbles from layer four will lose their energy as heat and bubble up to layers three and two. Sometime a bubble will go from layer four to two without losing any energy for some reason. Besides stimuli, tiny machines come in through the INPUT prong of the cables, scan the energetic levels, and exit the OUTPUT prongs, obviously creating a feedback loop of both artificial and actual reality, possibly. This is what They think happens. They might be right. This is the system that Elliott's mind has constructed for the operation and survival of itself. Elliott recreates the system with differing radii, heights, mediums, densities, cables, positioning systems, material of the cables, sources of structural disintegrity, stimuli, energetic states, machines, every two minutes.

(Dr. Karms exits the room. Elliott is still asleep)

(*Curtain*)

Still 1.18

Winter collects in the kidneys. Shadows flush. Glasses of dead water sit in all four corners of the room: calcium rings each all the way down. ART, protein, calcium, and other shit. Kidney pain stiffed by a wrist and a knuckle: it's a keeper. The bed is uncalm. Morning frees the fold of winter. Pain 1 inch down: twist and count all the plates I've ever chipped. My cock burns stiff: I fumble up a cup the size of 4 cups and try to piss. I dribble warm lithium yellow, cough it up, stones fall out. Some people suck stones: others piss them.

Hunger

I'm not hungry. Why put food in just to shit it out. Tubes might have
been explored earlier. No need to repeat. I can't remember the taste
of efficiency. What I wanted. I wanted? I can't remember the taste of
hunger. That's been said before, but it remains because it's true and
can't be reduced. Or maybe it hasn't been said. Hunger, stupid little
thing, haven't we evolved yet past that, no, a generalization, a blanket
statement, too shit stained, but at least warm. At the Motel, food was
neither there nor not. Food came when They felt like it: baggies of
protein, carbohydrates, vitamins, minerals, maybe some of the less
essential ones. When I was a child, the food came in bright, gold foil
much like the pills still do today. Nostalgia happens. Then something
changed and the food started coming in plastic baggies. The motives
behind the change are unknown and irrelevant. What is relevant is
the gold foil envelopes. I collected them as a child, didn't care what
was inside of them, I just wanted them. By the backdoor in the crawlspace, away from my mother's eyes, I stacked them shiny in piles of 15
everywhere in that concrete square and around the support columns.
After I meticulously ordered the foils, I would swim in them, scat-
tering them all over the cement floor. They were the closest things
to money I have ever seen because I've never seen it. I swam and
swam until my mother came and dragged me and my foils out of

the crawlspace. My mother would throw them at me or at my father, then my father would throw them back at my mother, and my mother would take one of the envelopes and cut all the webbing between my fingers. The punishments never deterred me. A long digression long: I'm not hungry. With my illness, They tell me to eat. They tell me by having four people enter with their bowl, ladle, powders and viscous liquids. I tell them I'm not hungry. They both listen and pretend to listen. However, They come back, breaking the silence of the room and mix Their psychedelic slop in front of my firmly trapped gullet. Their psychedelic slop bores me. "Can't you see I'm wallowing in my own boredom?" I say. They reply by sharpening Their ladle. At first I refused the slop firmly, then once, just once, I let the slop in. To my surprise, the slop placated me. Superfine placation: dulled me with sharp boredom: all the blood rushed to my stomach and the sharp boredom squatted down. The stimulation has built a threshold that cannot be broken. Now I let the four do whatever They want because They will do it anyway. I gnash my stomach at Them.

Vials

"Put your teeth on me," Preeti says. Elliott shifts from his seat at the kitchen table, opens his lips wide and presses his teeth to her lips, cracked with purple pockets. She turns her head side-to-side letting his teeth slide. The cracked skin runs along the bottom of his. His smile causes his lips to crack and sting. He laughs and pulls away, leaving red in the grooves of his front teeth. "You have red," – she taps her own teeth with her free hand – "lick." Elliott licks his teeth and sits back down at the table. The vials on the tabletop shake. He picks up Saint's needle and continues to fill the vials. He fills three, then picks up a white wax marker and draws a circle on each of them and puts them in a sock. Inside the vials, the bubbles rub red black up the glass. "Yours is fat. And cheap. Lighter at the bottom than the top," Preeti says, laughing, holding the vials to the light. "Fuck you," Elliott says, slightly smiling, "yours is AAA." "You never leave the house, and it shows, in these, your blood is stupid," she says, tapping a vial. "Why go out? You want to. Don't piss on my gate," he says. She goes back to putting the filled vials into the sock, bleached yellow with grey splotches of toes and a heel. She sits silent. A vial breaks and black red seeps near the toe. "Hope they go ape shit for this lot. I hope it saves their perfect kids and their perfect cunts," she says. Saint quietly stands in front of the stove stirring the old, used vials in a boiling pot of water. The fan hums oblong evaporation. He turns around, pulling off his ratty rubber glove. He wipes some sweat on his purple apron. He looks at the sock on the table. "Careful, it's not like that shit grows on us," – he smiles his broken smile – "waste not like the protein farmers, a surplus then they kill the pigs then feed them to the next lot," Saint says. Elliott puts down the needle on the table. He looks at Saint. "Why do you boil them before we fill them?" – Elliott stands up, moving to the stove – "pointless." "Looks. That's all." He puts on the glove again and pulls more vials out of the boiling water, placing them on a cloth on the counter, water evaporating from the cylinders, "No one likes a dirty vial". He smiles again and slides the glove back on.

Suck

Red swallows me in the back of a dead lot, all lots are dead lots, this is where it happens always, not going to change much. My back to brick, a square lot, all four walls brick, narrows to the right, night roots down above. I roll my head side-to-side, trying to crack the second in my neck. All four corners sprout street lamps with pairs of shoes tethered to them. The shoes twin forward, back, left and right at even rates. The light from the lamps leaks cheap. Red's hair and stubble shift forward thick red curls, soft as gravel: his mouth missing the two back molars top and bottom, absence on the underside of my cock, the remainders cut. Across the lot, twelve door frames lean against the wall, all ajar inwards, chipped, white. Some of the yellow lines stenciled on the pavement fade. Words are seldom exchanged in these situations. I'm not talking now because I don't want to. Red has a voice too, but he's not using it. Bass muffles through the brick. My neck can't crack now. Red's spit soaks into the zipper of my pants, my tubes tighten, air continues to chill the air. My neck cracks: ten fingers around Red's skull and neck tendons pulse: clench back and breathe. We carefully and mechanically shift positions. Light pollution bastards the night.

Still 1.13

Mother dies today: she sits upright, my head in her lap: a medical tube siphons blood out of her leg. Her hair is creased. Her eyebrows are creases. Her nose is a crease. Her eyes are creases. Her face is too creased. Her lips are too cobalt. Her neck is too tendon. She is too creased. I remember everything about her: I remember nothing about her. The medical tube pushes shadow hydrostatically from her leg into my wrists cut with her eyeglasses. On the floor, next to her still leg, a cup the size of 4 cups hides its busted handle under the bed. The cups holds ⅓ shadow. Another blanket wets its way on the bed from the wall. I try to count all the cankers in my mouth because teeth need shadows too. I get stuck between 6 and 7 and that's all.

BIRTHIVIDEBTUBEREMBERSCUDDERETRO
VIRUSALINECKLEPTONICOTINEPIVIRUSTA
TICTACTOESTERRORISMOCKETAMINERVE
NTRANCEMENTIMEATOMBOMBANGERMEN
ORVIRUSSIARTANKLEAKEROSENEMATODE
AFORTOVASEVERESCRIPTORGASMILEASH
ERTZERITEETHIVIDEXEDRINEEDLEDUSTA
INCRIXIVANUSIGILLNESSPERMAFROSTRA
INKILLAYARNASPARTAMEVIRACEPTRAPE
NGLISHITOWOMBEEPOWOMENICKIDEATH

Dear Karen Lehmann: or Kathy Acker: or Janey: or
Dr. Stranglelove or: How I Learned From You To Make Bombs,

I know you're dead and all, but people are still trying to kill you even though you died in '97. Men and women too because they are stupid and jealous and don't want to upset the googley eyes of status quo that keeps their comfort happening. There's only one copy of Empire at the University library and one copy of My Mother at the public. Nothing has changed since you died: children are stupid, can't read, and are too busy with their meth homework: I can't read anymore because I was never taught how to: adults can't read anymore because they're all dead. Western societies are now exceedingly credential-based and people shit on anything extra they have to read or do that gets in the way of them getting their cultural capital (DEGREE) including education. Once the good is acquired, there are no jobs anyway to apply it to. Only young business people who believe in infinite capital are trained by the old business people and then given jobs: self-fulfilling circle jerk. Education at all levels is about business now: PEPSI + PEPSI = 5: Vaseline can't be stuffed back into tubes ONLY INTO ASSHOLES. Because everything is now a business only business people survive. Only rich people can afford technological innovations and medicine and LIFE and shit on everyone else who can't. America still heaps recessions and DEATH upon the rest of the world. In Canada, people think your work stinks because it isn't beautiful and doesn't read like an inedible person trying to eat their own cock or cunt: CANNED LIT = AUTOEROTICISM. On a stained note: the oceans are cancer: the land is cancer: the sky is cancer. You died of breast cancer in '97 and many women I love will most likely die of it too because of that whole genetics thing and the earth is one giant polluted Petri dish: CLOSED SYSTEM: I get fear and become a weak microbe with sharp carbon monoxide in my eyes. You're one of the few who figured out this literal, figurative, economic, cultural, political *et al.* ways circle jerk. See you in Mexico Room 101 if the DRUG LORDS and AMERICAN NOSTRILS don't destroy it first.

Love,

Elliott

Still 1.15

I count every window that has ever looked at me: I stop at zero because it is stupid. Back door, no door thought it was a door, just a
window 4 large rectangle glass scratches stuffed pregnant with age.
Cobalt grass waves into the room: scratch and sniff air. A chair creases with clothing on it. Some chairs hold up people better than others.
The chair crowns the table. A man with unfamiliar ribs, ankles, and
cock leans on the chair; he spits relaxed into a fire barrel burning. The
Persian carpet under foot is burnt with rings. We sit on the carpet. No
talking just thinking because I want to. On the floor, all the spoons all
line up all and circle a pot that's never been used because its so white I
know this because it is white. All the spoons, tens of spoons, all stasis
around at even intervals.

Scars

My hands slide to Red's hips, fingers around the bulbs. Faint stretch marks thin around his hip. My fingers hold perfectly on his bones. His shoulder blades poke white skin except the right: a gasmask tattoo half-finished with freckles, curves down around the shoulder. Soft panting happens. Then grunting. Streetlight scuttles up the wall in weak lymph. I slide my hands down his thighs and bring them back up. He leans down. My penis bends inside him. I keep my hands there, coma moist. He grunts: shudders. Pubic hair is friction. I come and tighten. I pull out, slide off, and lie down. He lies facing away from me. To the window: wall: wallpaper. His back beads. Broken outline of the mask on his blade wraps down his shoulder: bubbles of blood ink. His pale skin blurs the ink. The streetlight snags on his red hair. I touch his hips, he shifts stiff. "Who inked you?" I ask, rubbing the bubbles. Silence: lice: ice crystals on the corner of the window, a stalled crescent tall arched yellow. Low breaths, then silence. "I did. Did what I could by myself. Got someone to finish the rest. Fucked up some places, bad, bubbles, barbed it," – he shifts to face me, his white teeth sharpened by dark – "still got the gun, homemade, cassette motor, long-ass needle, old cord. You should let me get you," – he rubs over the bubbles, adjusts the blanket. I rub my thumb along the bubbles, press them, hard. "The fuck-ups felt good, all pins and needle like, like them more than the mask now," – he stretches – "Got any cloth?" He sits upright on the mattress, looking around the floor. "There should be," I say. I look around my side, around the ashtrays. A couple of scraps limp out under the mattress. I pull out two and hand them to him. He wipes his asshole and tosses them to the floor and gets back into bed. "What about your scars?" – his fingers stroke my cheek.

"A sleep," I say. "Shit. Sleep did that, glad I cut it," he says. We laugh. He shifts and looks at me. "Where's your girl?" he says. "Don't know," I say. "How long she gone?" he says. "A couple days," I say. "Hope she comes back alright," I say. "Yeah," I say. "Do you think it exists," he says. "No," I say. "Forty-sixty, for me," he says. Silence. His arm tightens. He smells of chlorine. His toenails dig into my leg. Outside, a truck drives by, cutting the night.

Still 1.12

Every complex on every street in the City has a steel T on its apex: no one knows what the T means because everyone does. Every subsection of the complex has three windows, some more boarded than others. Under the apex, in the overhang, wasps graft a nest in the shape of the complex it is attached to and wait for the garbage to grow below.

The Road

is shit and bone and molars and cigarette butts and asphalt and Coke cans for a touch of aesthetic. I walk in the middle of it because there is no other reason. My legs can't keep up with the yellow lines. I've tried, but I can't keep up and that's ok. The sky fattens blue: the wind slurs feral: the clouds tweek. I've been walking for minutes, hours, don't know: dramatic. I look back on the road and I can maybe, no, I can't see the Motel, all pixilated now in focus but still nothing. I don't know why I left. No. I do know. Preeti hasn't been home in nights. And days. Both are too loud. There are other reasons I'm sure. No. But it doesn't matter. At the end of the road is a wall made of concrete four stories solid, uneven pour knots like a concrete floor, vanishing points in either direction. To the right of the road, there's a crack 7m tall, top skinny, bottom fat, a spraypainted outline around the edges bone white outlined by strontium red. I pick up a rock and huck it through the crack. After hearing the rock hit the ground, I slip into the crack, snag my shoulder on a chainlink layer. I shuffle out the crack left and get back on the road. I walk for an hour. I know it's an hour this time and get bored. It's night now. Since I'm bored, I look up at the stars because they are as bored as I am. Backward, the City spikes a popped bubble of light pollution. I lie down on the road right on a yellow line, spread my arms and legs and make an X. I play stitch for 10 minutes, feeling the fabric of the road, pinch at it. I get bored so I walk again. I walk under a bridge. After the bridge, the hills flatten and the forest fattens and darkens. In a ditch, there's a mailbox upright. Inside the mailbox there's nothing because I check: I kick: I shake. I pick up the rocks around it and put them in the box for no reason. I root around in the trees for more: I find more and haul them and stuff them in because there is no reason. I fill it and go back to the road. It's morning somehow. I see a something coming from the City. I see a car coming from, no, a truck coming from the City reddening in the morning heat. It reddens because it is one of those big red rusted trucks. I wait in the middle of the road with all my fingers out because I forget which one to stick out. The truck downshifts kilometres away. It stops 100m down. I walk back towards it. On the side of the road, I pocket a fist-sized rock in my jacket. I'm wearing a jacket, a hot denim jacket, I didn't know was so hot. This detail should have been mentioned earlier. Details leak. The truck's cab is high. The door swings open, springs the hinges, and slams shut. The door opens for a second time, springs the hinges: I catch the side, hop up and in. The seats are covered in plastic baggies with white powder over the ripped vinyl. The whole cab smells of bleach. The driver leans back into the corner: little bald wedged face, black eyes, teeth chatter. "Where are you going to," he says. "Dead Man's Flats, never been that far out West," I say. This detail should have been mentioned earlier. Details leak. "Why are you going?" he says. "I don't remember," I say. "Why don't you remember?" he says. I shut the door. "A vacation," I say. "Why don't you remember," he says. "I just told you. Why don't you remember?" I say. "Yes. Yes you did," he says. He starts the engine and the whole cab fills with silence. He begins to drive, still looking at me. "My name is Arms," he says. "I'm a driver because I'm driving. You're a hitchhiker because you're a hitchhiker," he says. "I'm Steve," I say. "That's not your name," he says. "Yes it is. Is your name really Arms?" I say. "Yes it is," he says. We sit in silence as the hood of the truck snorts the yellow lines. "Where are you going?" I say. "Lac des Cars.

The lake with the carbohydrate plant. I am going to 'fill her up,'" he says. He uses those stupid hand signs. His eyes beam with something. "Never seen it," I say. "It's an old lake with an old quarry dug into it that still digs into the mountain," he says. I don't know what to say, so I don't reply. No, I know what to say. "So everyone in the City eats mountain?" I say. He sweats and his teeth chatter. "No, uh, not, not exactly. The mountain is one of many powders mixed in becoming fit for consumption," he says. He sounds so stupid I just zone out and look out the window. The pine trees are plastic-mâchéed with white bags. The sun eats down from overhead. "Are we there yet?" I say. "Almost. 5 to 6 minutes," he says. We pass through a gauge in the mountain. Every fractured face in the rock has a tombstone stenciled on it with black spraypaint. We dip down a hill. For some reason he downshifts at the bottom and we lurch forward. After the mâchéed trees, we pass a lake with what looks like an industrial plant, metal tubes, and exhaust the same size and slope of the mountain behind it. The lake water shifts cobalt stuffed with half-submerged cars. Next to the plant, a gigantic sign reads: CARBOHYDRATES. "Is that your plant?" I say. "No," he says. I'm not going to talk to him anymore. We continue past the plant and pass a hill made of loose chain link fencing. While going up a hill, he tries to shift gears but instead grabs my leg. I pull my rock on him. He cowers, then seems to forget about the whole thing. We pass under a bridge that's missing: we pass under a skylight. We pass a shotgunned sign: MAN FLAT. We take an off-ramp and come to a burned-out gas station. The parking lot is filled with burned-out vehicles with grass and other flowers growing outside on the frames. The trees in the valley are all burned bone white smooth. The ground is green and black. No houses anywhere, only piles of rusted vents and water heaters. "Watch out for incendiaries," he says. I get out of the truck, Arms watching me in his heat. He slams the door and drives still heading West. I walk into the gas station, the grass creeps up the door. The door slides open automatically without a ting, burnt caulking falls off the frame. Inside everything is burnt.

Sun steams in through the broken windows walls ceiling holes. My eyes adjust to the burn. The counter is burnt. The walls are burnt. The coolers are burnt melted plastic. I walk behind the cash register and piss. After I piss, my bowels tick. I take a shit behind the register. I open the register and pull out a road map, only an inch burnt by the staples and wipe my ass. The paper breaks apart: specks stick around my asshole. I rise and see that there's a restaurant connected, equally burnt-out. The tables hug the broken windows, all mossed over. The tiles are melted. The candy machines bubble black broken. The centre island booths are burnt still and jagged. The booths near the kitchen wall are burnt, but smooth. I find a booth by the kitchen and sit, the black vinyl cracks. I brush off the ash, lay down and sleep. I wake up; it's night. I can't distinguish between the burnt and the dark, so I go back to sleep. I wake up in the morning and walk around. I check the kitchen for food: nothing. I check the freezer: there's only four aluminum walls and no roof. I close the door and walk back out and look out the window by one of the mossed tables. In the car, moss covers a burnt skeleton melted into the driver's side. I turn around and survey the burnt. This place sucks. I go back to the booth and put my hands on the burnt backrest, now nothing but a cracked membrane. After making three handprints on it, I fall asleep again. I wake up and assume it's night and fall back asleep because there is nothing to do. I wake up again and it's morning, early morning, its moist and hot and sunny to me. I adjust my eyes to the burn and stumble to the front door: it slides open: the bright sun flooded. I'm hungry and thirsty and bored: I decide to go home. It starts to rain suddenly so I open my mouth. I drink for a few minutes, then the rain stops: the rain tastes of Iso. I walk up the off-ramp, down off the off-ramp, and up the grass hill. The water evaporates off the grass, trees and pavement. The whole valley burns in evaporation. I fall twice, each time slipping all the way back down to the bottom of the grass hill. My pants and shirt are soaked: they dry in a minute. My jacket is lost: it was shit anyway. My ass itches, most likely from the specks of paper stuck to it. At the top of the dry road, I piss. The piss evaporates, leaving sulphur yellow puddles on the asphalt. I look West: nothing but sticks, BONE SHARP STUPID STICKS. No more road or lines or anything – just sticks. Sticks sprawl the road and the grass on either side of it. I say sticks because I mean it. Nothing but sticks next to each other, crisscrossing each other, some more perpendicular than others. In fact, a lot more sticks perpendicular than anything, sharp stupid around and over the hill. The tips of the sticks darken violet in the sun. I attempt to walk through the sticks, unbalanced, eyeing the perpendicular ones. I get a step or two in, then turn around. The sun sets on the mountaintop and bands through the evaporation. I start to walk East because that was my original plan. The valley darkens. I don't know why I stepped into the sticks like that. The reason is unknown but I'm happy to have done it. I walk for an hour in the middle of the road for no reason. The heat from the day leaves. My feet grope by the yellow lines. Every once in a while, I take a nap by the girders. After twelve naps, I'm still tired and haven't reached the MAN FLAT sign. I keep walking in the dark. I hear downshifting behind me. I turn and it looks like another red truck because it is a red truck. I throw out all five fingers on my hand like before. The truck comes to me and breaks. The door swings open, springs the hinges, and shuts. The door opens for a second time slower and stays open. I hop up and into the cab. It's that Arms guy again. "Are you going back already?" he asks. "Yeah. The West was a dump," I say. He starts driving.

Commercial 5 – How to Explain Dead Alive Images to the Dying (I Like ACMERICA and ACMERICA Likes Me)

(President DEAD *appears standing in front of the bed, dressed as* Joseph Beuys, *his head anointed with Cubic Zirconias and Dr. Pepper, his feet jammed into compressed air canisters. He's cradling a skinned* Bugs Bunny. *An anemic, albino* Wylie Coyote *circles the two: foam drips from his mouth and burns into centipedes on the floor*)

President DEAD: Entheogens and other spiritual practices are dead like this fucking rabbit. Don't mind that coyote circling the daily diary of the American dream. We've been placating him with numerous ACME inventions for years: I'm just about to hook him onto the Spade and huck him into St. Nowhere. We have not yet looked into the rebirth rituals and will most likely not in the near future as it is hippy shit. Egocide (death) noun [C or U]: Intentional killing of the ego is frowned on. Wide definitions would include martyrdom and self-sacrifice; narrower definitions are negligible because all cases are frequently considered cowardly and insane by us: egocide is a common object of moral prohibition. According to us: bodily energy lattices DO NOT exist: Certain art forms DO NOT resonate with certain chakra or energy centres: we often don't know anything except control, we only deal with control. The capacity to reactivate these torpored forces has been shot to shit because of us: as man becomes dormant, through technology etc., the animal heightens. As I started living in my own technological realm, it became a new nature to me and I started destroying the coyote's straw bedding (NATURE). I even loaned that ungrateful shit ACME technology to better acclimatize to my new nature, but it only pissed and chewed on it because all the ACME technology is shit anyway and just flashy squeak toys.

(APPLAUSE)

Coyote: I HATE ACMERICA AND ACMERICA HATES ME. THEY HATE ME BECAUSE I EAT OBESE BABIES THAT ROLL OFF THE SETS OF TALK SHOWS BECAUSE THERE ARE NO MORE WILD ROADRUNNERS OR RABBITS. THIS ASSHOLE KILLED THE LAST ONE IN HIS ARMS DEAD. HE JUST KEEPS GIVING ME THESE SHIT DEVICES THAT DON'T DO DICK. I WANT TO CARBON MONOXIDE MYSELF. CAPITALISM CANNIBALIZES EVERYTHING. NOTHING IS SAFE, NOT EVEN ART. CAPITALISM EATS WHERE IT SLEEPS WHERE IT FUCKS WHERE IT SHITS: I DON'T EVEN DO THAT.

(BOOS)

President DEAD: By the 20th century, egocide was diagnosed as the result of either psychological illness (Freud) or the pressures of social conditions (Durkheim). Egocide prohibition was strong in the early Freudian-Christian tradition because Freud needed the ego to hock his ointment: THANK THE G-O-DOUBLE-D's. Egocide is now uncommon in other cultures where egocide in various circumstances was institutionally embedded because we've killed them NONENTITY. Scientists and medical staff at our facilities possess psychotherapeutic and technologic training to ensure that our elite have something to entertain themselves with.

(President DEAD *gathers Fillet-O-Fish wrappers from his pockets to create a cube around himself. His body pixelates to the point of obscurification. From a top corner of this sudden microchip, an antenna extends crooked. A flashlight turns on inside and he continues to speak*)

President DEAD: "Just as the human body, aided by a protective skin of wax paper and transfats is naturally engineered to heal itself, our future hinges on transmission towers, Wall Street, and the eradication through perpetuation of non-Theys. FYI: THE CURE doesn't exist and if it was created, ACME would ensure it would never work: it's stuck in a vial sitting under a cracking, gravity deifying, red rock overhang in a yellow desert under a yellow sky.

(APPLAUSE)

President DEAD: The rabbit is the second most easily skinned mammal on earth. The ban on egocide was fortified in the middle ages and became a sissy fight between Enlightenment thinkers, notably Hume, and conservatives such as Kant, an antenna – part-abiotic sage, part-consumptive capitalist worldview. Kant couldn't foresee that too much sublime could be detrimental as it leads to overstimulation and numbness. As we curb-stomped nature dead meat and replaced it with technology – our own brand of nature – the sublime mutated: object of nature melds to the human mind: PARALYSIS = CLUSTER FUCK. As technology becomes more micronized you know what they say: MO' MICRO MO' PROBLEMS. Have to repack the skull. In places like St. Nowhere, we provide a last-minute cathartic yet reassuring technological slough to locate both the psychological trauma and pleasure points of the nucleus of personal histories via the Spade, one of ACME's finest inventions. After years of having a technological surplus means to ensure They's long, healthy existence and a deficit in good art, we decided that the only artful thing left is death. An awakening perception of the intolerable ways the medical profession had managed death helped us catalyze this observation of the large pool of resources in front of us. We engineered the HIV virus, then spread it to ensure the spectacle of death for decades to come. An art gallowery, if you will.

(Coyote *rips apart the Fillet-O-Fish microchip and cracks the neck of* President DEAD *with its jaws.* Coyote *drags* President DEAD *in his jaws around the room until he stops twitching and/or drowns in centipedes.*)

(Curtain)

Stairs

Preeti can't make it up the stairs. Knees needle left unattended. Her laughter up the stairwell. Her knuckles tuck around the banister. The K stutters from her teeth. Through the black, the light tightens under the door. Hair tangled, blood leaks from her nose. She lies down at the top of the stairs outside of Saint's door. Her eyes titter back into her skull: fingers open and contract.

She lies down in the bed. I'm already there. She tries to tuck her hand under my blanket, through the folds trying to unspiral them. "I errored. I can't remember, where I went, pitting," she says. "I know where you went. Then and Now. You don't even know where you went," I say. "That's not true. I went." – she freezes, her eyes titter back in her skull, – "Where did I go?" she says. "You don't want to know," I say. "Tell me," she says. "You went pitting," I say. "Tell me," she says. "Pits are where people get gang fucked to get THE CURE, maybe, lots of guys, a couple of girls, knives, cutting too," I say. "Have you ever seen?" she says. "No," I say. "I understand why I didn't know where I went," she says. "No, you don't," I say. "You always stay here, there are other places to go, and think about," she says. "I like this place. Didn't go out much. I like it here. It's all a pit outside," I say. The rooms-lightens into pale blue, then pulses three times. Her chest inflates and deflates. The cuts on her brown skin inflate and deflate. Her blood rolls off like mercury. "It doesn't exist does it?" I say. "No, it doesn't exist," – she turns and curls her legs up over me – "What do you want me to do," she says. "Sleep," I say. "You know sleep won't happen," she says. "Do whatever you do," I say. She gains weight: the mattress sags. Her eyes titter back into her skull. "Sleep Elliott," she says. Inside the room, the morning wrings itself dry.

Food 1.3

Four hands stacked, four hands fat hold a clear bowl in front of my face. The ladle drops a dollop of melted Vaseline, ripples up the curves, loosens steam. "Dollop," a he says. The ladle pulls up. Above, a hand cracks a white packet of white salt in the middle of the bowl, ripples the surface. The hand cracked packet pulls up. A half sphere of red in the middle. Clear gel still circles on the outside. "Enough," says another he. Blue rectangles flutter down, some stick to the sides of the bowl and clot. "Dab," another he says. Some rectangles ripple the liquid and spider blue to the bottom of the bowl. "Poke," a she says. Her fingers powdered yellow grid the surface and clot. The she bites her pinkie nail, sucks off the powder. All four people slowly back up and out the room. The bowl slips off my chest, off the bed, and spills on the floor.

PPM

Saint gets up from the mattress and pulls up his pants: crotch holes all over, frayed, just a muscle shirt. He rubs his skull into a yawn, reaches into his back pocket for his smokes, pulls out the package, aged with creases. Takes one out, all tapeworm, lights it curved. One of his eyes struggles to open. Stubble on chin. Red and Elliott lie on the mattress on the floor. The width of Saint apart. The afternoon sun leaks through the window above their heads. Dust and hair hover in the air. Red's eyelids titter. Face up. He licks the stubble above his lips. The red of his hair rubs off onto the mattress. Elliott lies quietly, trying to sleep. The mattress has no cover. Lice play dead around the legs. The blankets smell of headache. The sun leaves thick smears wherever it lands: pale blue and yellow. Saint touches the mirror and slides his fingers together, rubs the sun around. He lifts up his muscle shirt and rubs the sun above his belly button, velcros to his stomach hairs. "Nice tummy," says Elliott, still lying down, blocking out the reflection of the sun with his hand. "Shit, light feels warm," says Saint, laughing, flashes him his stomach. "What's the time?" Elliott says. "Not sure," – he scratches his armpit – "afternoon, don't matter." Elliott lies still. Saint picks up a pair of scissors out of an ashtray, shakes the ash off. He shuffles through the piles of clothes and baggies. His one naked foot limps on the wood. The other foot socked silent. Into the hall, left into the bathroom. The bathroom door sways open. Saint reaches for the lightbulb string, pulls four times, catches on the fourth. Saint stands facing the mirror, belly to the basin. The mirror stained with the door's reflection. The lightbulb tightens overhead. Saint leans over the basin to the mirror, cleans sleep out of his eyes, crooks his neck back to see up his nostrils, looks for loose cocaine. He takes his scissors and snips: little staggers of frost coarse black. He sucks them. He tosses the scissors down on the soap dish: half-dried bubbles brace it crooked. A plastic bottle of colloidal silver spills on the ground: 10ppm: the PM meats. Wet eats at his toes on the tiles. He looks at his stubble, cracks his mouth, fingers his teeth for bleeding, picks up the scissors on the soap dish, opens the blades, brings them to his neck. The blades never meet, repetition is necessary. His penis dribbles through his jeans. On his neck, the two red lines meet. He lies down on the cold tiles, slumps old: eye water stuck in his wrinkles. Spit dribbles from his mouth: ache red. Red still sleeps, rubs more red on the mattress. Elliott's eyes titter. The sheets crisp and snap; Elliott shifts under the pieces and over his head. Under the sheets, Elliott rubs the stitches on Red's chest: soft breasts: stitchings zigzag, start at nipple level, spirals around each breast, fray with orange yarn, naps, twists, pokes up. Elliott runs his tongue over the stitches spiral outwards. Red still sleeps still. From under the covers, the sunlight, pregnant, topples with ache. Red smiles in his sleep: inches of stitch: cheek to cheek.

Still 1.17

I sit naked on the edge of a table, a deck of cards stack perfectly behind my ass. Ground is not meant to be reached by legs. The wood of
the table hasn't seen sand. One card opens face spade up. A glass of
water sits to the right of the card. A glass of water tastes better when
you ignore it.

Commercial 6 – ART of Darkness

(*On a freighter off the coast of South-East America*)

The Director of Corporations was the bitch and host. The other three people affectionately watched his ass while he rubbed his cock looking seaward. Besides encouraging simultaneous arousal in the three, it had the effect of making the three of them aware of each other's yearns – and even convictions. The Lawyer – the best of old Republicans – was because of his many victims lying rug burnt in the sun. The PEPFAR accountant had brought out a box of abstinence and was licking architecturally the bones. Marrow sat cross-legged right on top of left, then left on top of right then right on top of left, leaning against the rear mast stroking his cock. He had high cheeks, a swollen complexion, a straight back, an aseptic aspect and, with his arms dropped, the palms of his hands outward, resembled a plastic Buddha toy. The Director satisfied the anchor, he flicked his semen into the water and made his way over and sat down. They exchanged a few words. Afterwards there was silence finally. They did not begin that game of dominoes as no one knew what dominoes were. They felt medicated and fit for nothing but plastic staring. The day was ending in a sterile and exquisite boredom. The water sharpened peacefully. The sky was a speck of benign endometrium in confused light. The very mist was gauzy. Only the shotgun blasts to the West breeding over the upper reaches became more frequent every minute, as if angered by the approach of an orphaned son.

Dreams: Seeds: Germs of the Empire.

Marrow started talking and did not shut up.

Marrow: "This had been one of the brightest ideas from America. I was thinking of very recent times, when Americans first came here, 30 years ago – yesterday. Engineered the virus, spread it, then condos, Wal-Marts, and then the smiley democracy. What saves us personally is our inefficiency – the devotion to inefficiency. But these Americans, they were biocolonialists and for that you don't want brute force – nothing to toast off, when you have released it, since your capital and wealth is just a gun accident arising from the weakness of others' immune systems. Then they capitalized on what they found sitting around and sent it home or abroad to increase the GDP. It was robbery without violence, suicide with a swallowed cord, men going blind, darkness tackling them. The conquest of foreign lands, which means stealing it from those with different alleles, is a shiny thing and we should look at it. What creams it is the idea. The idea, dry up the back of it. An idea unprotected and lubricated. The selfish belief in the idea – something you can stick, and bob up and down on, and offer a line of cocaine to...."

Marrow removed his cock from his pants and started to jerk off. Gasoline gunshotted on the river, small reptile green holes on the surface, red sulphur shavings, plastic baggies, stalking, teething, screwing, breaking each other – then sinking. The light pollution of Congo City leaked out into the deaf night upon the bruised canals. We looked at Marrow, waiting patiently for him to come – there was nothing to entertain til the semen trickled down his shaft; but it was only after a long spasm, when he said in a clicking pilot light voice, "I suppose I should tell you a story about a dead, white man that happened in the jungle over there," that we knew, we were going to be spoken at for hours about one of Marrow's stupid experiences.

Marrow: "When I was a little shit, I had a passion for nothing as

I was never allowed to go to school as there were none. I spent all day in a collapsed stripmall that took the shape of a nest of I-beams, chainlink fence, tetanus, pink insulation, shadows, yarn, matchsticks, old pornography, stolen cigarettes, mice, dead mice, mice burning on sticks, shadows, fire, masturbation, and a copy of Milton's 'Paradise Lost' from which I learnt all my English, that's why I fucking rule. I would put my hand on the book and say: If I don't die, I want to squat there. I didn't die and grew up to be a bigger piece of shit that sucked off high-ranking Theys through chainlink glory holes. Their ten ivory fingers stroking my hair through the chain-links in little circles, pushing my lips and teeth and tongue into the rust when they came, then tossing me a bag of ART. My first meeting with the Manger was tiring. He made me walk back and forth over a thirty mile chain-link fence before he put his cock in my mouth. His features were uncommon: tiny, obsidian eyes too close together, stained filed teeth, black and grey matted hair with the consistency of soiled pornography, drunk, neck skin that hung like mouse fat, drunk, ears, and a YALE sweater. He was an international killer and a biocolonialist. He smiled and I didn't remember it. While I was sucking him, he asked if I wanted to go to Congo City to steal stuff and hock it to support North America. I guess I must have accidently nodded more left-to-right instead of up and down given the dick in my mouth because he jabbed my eye with his thumb. I yelped, then agreed. He put his cock back in my mouth and we resumed. Before he came, he muttered the following:

Manger: "GRAVES ... GRAVES ... story broken ... Mr. Hertz ... true ... NOT ... true ... so, uh, how do I know, uh, if I, uh, am getting, uh, the best picture ... are there machetes included? No GUNS ... I went further in and became part of the FIGHT ... hard to say, goodnight ... I can help too ... uh oh, there's one more ... dinosaur that goes on top ... Cheers, I ate some of my hair ... I spent 700 dollars on my cake ... I hope it pays off ... Pregnancy ... five days earlier ... flaming success ... I don't give a rat's ass about your social life ... HERTZ ... the stone is always picked up before it's cast ... we can't make bad drivers go away … girls don't have Adam's apples … seen any ghosts here? … even you, yeah you look into my eyes….

"I gathered it was something about a man named Hertz and something called cake. After swallowing his ejaculate, I asked him: "Who the fuck is Hertz?" "The chief of Habitornull, a multinational corporation given 7.01 billion dollars in contracts to spruce up the Congo," he said in a tone. He picked his nails for a while. "He is a porn star," he said coolly. "He is a disseminary of the American way, and technology, and pathology, and God knows what else. We want," he wept suddenly, "for the guidance of our destiny given to us by God." I told him I didn't know what God was. He told me it's the thing written in money. I asked him what was money. He poked me in the eye. I fell over. After I got up, the Manger told me that Hertz wasn't returning any of his calls and that he feared him sick or dead or fucking someone else. He wanted to know how long it would take me to get there. I told him I didn't know what Congo City was. He jabbed me in the eye again. I fell over. I blacked out.

"The next day, I woke up on a USS Kidd (DDG 993) Destroyer travelling over the Atlantic Ocean. Originally built for Iran, these ships became operational on July 27, 1981. The previous sentence was whispered in my ear as I was being raped by two Marines in the hull next to crates of sawdust. After they were finished, they water boarded me with their piss. I passed out again.

"The next day, I woke up and crawled up from the hull. My shirt and eyelids were starched with urine and semen. On the deck, I watched two Marines have sex in the cockpit of a F-14A Tomcat. From the moans, I ascertained their names were Mauvedick and Liceman, although which name belonged to which Marine I didn't catch or care to catch, as all Marines and military personnel are now self-willingly interchangeable excess units of human capital. After they finished, I heard the following exchange:

Liceman: "You're my Cowboy."

Mauvedick: "What's your damage, Lice. Wanna play Doom 3?"

Liceman: "You're my problem. It is so fucking sexy when you take out your big top-less gun and compromise the sovereignty of a weaker nation TITS UP YUM. You're safe. I like you because you're dangerous."

Mauvedick: "I'm glad you like me feeding you (Strokes his nose). HEY. WHAT THE FUCK IS THAT?!! (He pointed at me from the cockpit) WHY, THAT'S THAT LITTLE WIND SCORPION WE WERE SANDBAGGIN' DOWN IN THE HULL!!!! HEY FAGGOT, COME HERE, QUIT WATCHIN' US! PAX AMERICANA!"

Mauvedick jumped from the cockpit, or was it Liceman who jumped from the cockpit. I can't really remember. I'll assume it was Mauvedick that jumped down first. Mauvedick popped a gel cap of pure MDMA and a little blue diamond-shaped Viagra pill and proceeded to choke and rape me again while Liceman videotaped it with his iPhone. While raping me, he hummed "Anger Zone" on loop. After his cock softened, he tossed me back in the hull into a crate of sawdust. He tried pissing on me again, but his piss was crooked as it was post-sex piss: it showered on his gold-toed boot and trickled into the darkness. Seeing that he missed pissing on me, he cursed then cracked a can of Budweiser and poured it on my swelling black throat with trained trajectory.

"The next day, I woke up and puked out bile sawdust pubic hair and passed out.

"The next day, I woke up on a steamship called something so stupid I forgot it. On our voyage, we enlisted a few fine methheads for a crew: trails of finely broken crystal meth lured them onto the ship from the surrounding forest. They were men who never stopped working to sleep or eat or shit or screw and were, in turn, ideal and expendable human capital. And as the voyage proceeded, they didn't kill each other in front of my face: each of the methheads had in its body a store of methamphetamines that came bubbling up to the surface in the forms of scabs which could be picked off at any time and smoked or eaten. In this boat, like all modern factories, the scabs

157

smoked themselves. When one methhead killed another methhead, the victor would dig out the scabs and toss the body in the river, to be picked apart by fish and birds and other creepy crawlers. The cuts in their arms made such a pleasant aroma for my face holes. The crew, after the initial skirmishes and petty rubbings, were as follows:

Alan Bhundy:

Back in North America, Alan was a shoe-picker. He would spend 9–2 picking shoes in a collapsed bus terminal. One day, he broke his ankle scavenging and through the accident, inadvertently became a better shoe-picker, as he was closer to the ground. He considers his accident to be the point of his success. He reminisces on the accident quite fondly. He had a wife, who was also his daughter, and a dog, but they all disappeared. He didn't miss them. His breath smelled like feet and his feet smelled like cavities. He walked around the deck of the boat with his hand down his ass-crack.

Vasquez Solaris:

The only competent crew member on board. Armed with box cutters, she could cut up a methhead in four minutes. She was clean with dreadlocks and dark skin. In the jungle, she planned on creating a society for cutting up methheads. She had expressed on numerous occasions she will kill me too, simply because I was a "WASPy male fuck." Even today I have the utmost faith in her.

Dan Black:

The resident mystic of the vessel who looked like an overdosed model complete with a skinny, nosebled mustache. Back in North America, he was a travelling shaman who traversed the Pacific Northwest in a bus that was converted into a chapel made of crushed aluminum cans. His communion involved feeding GHB to teenagers, then performing "The Despondent Copulation." He had two common activities onboard the boat. His first activity involved jerking off onto a single Post-It from a vast stockpile somewhere in his quarters, then smearing the semen into an archaic sigil that always turned out to look like the Chrysler logo. He then posted the note on the wall and waited for the river air to dry it. Once dry, he would light it on fire and chant. The second activity involved his sniper rifle, which he called Zarathustra. On several occasions, he made the rest of the crew call him the "Time Sniper." If a crewmember refused, he became agitated and pointed Zarathustra in his or her general direction and threatened to pump an "ER" in him or her. Often, the barrel jammed and nothing happened.

"Vasquez eventfully slit Black's throat and left him bleeding to death on the mind-burnt deck. The mosquitoes wandered down to the watering hole. There were other crewmembers, but they're not important because they're dead.

"We continued up the Congo River, but there were more bends busted, so we called it the Elbow River because we are American and we can do whatever the fuck we want to.

"Civilization begins with a river: a river is a plastic is a molecule is a polymer is a human is a tissue is a cell is a tumor is a death is a nothing: it continues with the booms, then thickens.

"The concrete floodwalls seemed inhuman. We are used to looking on the shaved form of a tranquilized simian, but here – in the concrete you could still imagine the earth behind it. No, no, you couldn't.

"After weeks, we finally reached a compound and we assumed it was Hertz's, for no good reason except all the cars parked along the river. The riverbank was dull: the trees were dull: the sky was dull: the air was dull. Once on the shore, Vasquez dropped Alan's body in the mud and I disembarked. I told her to watch the steamer and she told me that she was going to sharpen her box cutters. I started walking up the slope towards the compound. The ground was blistered with pine needles and acorns and frost. From the top of the hill, a transformer rolled halfway down before arcing sideways into the bush. I came to a large ball of power lines that were dead and tangled beyond recognition. Inside the centre of the ball, there was nothing. In the shady spot to the left, nothing stirred. No horns could be heard and no one was running. At the top of the slope, there were trailers, punctured propane canisters, and collapsed transmission lines.

"A slight silence behind me made me rotate 180 degrees. On the ground there were twelve cardboard boxes of earth and six loincloths. Under the boxes and loincloths there were six skeletons collared together with chains. I passed a tank wrapped in chain-link fencing and hoar-frost: the whole apparatus looked like bone. I kept walking. I walked down a path on a terraced hillside. On one of the steps, someone with a hose was watering fields of wind-rolled, plastic chrysanthemums. In the distance, I saw a white man shoot himself. I walked a little further into the compound. In the adjacent forest, I saw another white man trying to cut off his head with scissors. I'm hard as fuck but the life that I was tossed into blew. I've sucked the angel of silence, top shelf Theys, and the hot barrel of a gun, but by all the stars on the flag – fuck. As I stood on the hillside, I saw that in the flabby sun, down the hill there was a suburb made of trailers. For a moment I looked relieved. I descended the hill by tumbling down it.

"At the bottom, I avoided a medium-sized hole half-dug; stuck inside was a transformer tits-up in the air.

Then I nearly fell into another hole containing a USPS truck.

Then I nearly fell into another hole containing thousands of computer monitors.

Then I nearly fell into a hole filled with stripped circuit boards.

Then I nearly fell into a hole of phone cords.

The digging of the holes might have been connected with the sadistic core within capitalism to give white people somewhere to dump their shit. I didn't have a purpose, so I sat down in the shade. The rapids were near and stunk and shifted like mercury because they were mercury.

"Nothing crouched, lay, sat between the trees, leaned against the trunks, clung to the earth, half-coming out, half-erected with the dumb light in all the attitudes of silence and nothing. There were no eyes under the trees. There was no face near my hand. Nothing reclined at full length with one shoulder against the tree. No eyelids rose and no eyes looked up at me. Near the same tree, there were no bundles of angles with legs drawn. Nothing walked on all fours to the stagnant pond to drink. I walked into the centre of the trailer park.

"I had to wait in the compound for two days. To pass the time, I organized all the waste wires according to colour: white to red to green to blue to black and size: small to small-medium to medium to medium-large to large. On the third day, a small man who looked like Huckleberry Hound, only anemic and old and white, came to the centre with a stool and a notepad. Fat mosquitoes rolled around in the air. The forest started coughing. "The sick sharpen my attention," he said, "they are the biggest errors in this climate." He wrote on one of his pages, tore it, then handed it to me. I took it in my hand and read it:

MISTER HERTZ DEAD. NATIVES KILLED HIM LONG AGO. ASSHOLE. GO HOME. LOLZ

"He started writing again. The forest started coughing again. He screamed at the forest to shut up. He started writing again. The forest became too ill to cough. All the leaves frosted. The mosquitoes played dead.

"I went back to my hut and sorted some more wire. I heard gunshots outside and I saw the note giver bleeding in the dust. I knew I had to get out of there. I ran back to the boat. Vasquez was still sharpening her box cutters. We went back up the river. She stabbed me three times over the return voyage, failing each time to kill me. I dropped her off in the jungle. Before parting, she tried to stab me again. She tried to stab me four times over the return voyage. I wished her the best of luck and she reciprocated.

Fin."

Marrow stopped and sat scratching at the dried semen on his pants in the position of a bloated lotus. The Director of Corporations removed his pistol and shot him. He fell on the deck and then the Director kicked him over the edge into the water.

Going up the neural river was like traveling back to the earliest beginnings of the world. We the vegetation rotted on the earth and the big kings were trees.

A hollow axon: a silent roar: tundra.

The air was armless, slick, light and dumb.

There is joy in the dullness of sunshine.

Still 1.07

The room darkens cobalt. A lightbulb descends from the ceiling above the origin in the centre of the floor. An unfamiliar arm rises from the origin, elbow vertical, forearm falls naturally towards the window on the right, resting state. The radius of the arms reach varies in accordance with arm extension and contraction. The average radius is 1 metre. Quadrants glow. Quadrant 1: a metre up to the door, $\pi/2$, counterclockwise right angle a meter to the wall on the left, π. Quadrant 2: a metre to wall, π, counterclockwise right angle a metre to the foot of the bed, $3\pi/2$. Quadrant 4: a metre to the foot of the bed, $3\pi/2$, counterclockwise right angle a metre to the window on the right, 2π. Quadrant 1: a metre to the window on the right, 2π, counterclockwise right angle a metre up to the door, $\pi/2$. The arm falls naturally to 2π. A large mason jar filled with carbohydrate or protein or vitamin or mineral or sodium bicarbonate or sodium hypochlorite powder or water rests on π. The mason jar's lid rests at $\pi/2$. The arm contracts, hand down to the origin. The arm's hand extends to 2π. The hand feels up the arc into Quadrant 1 forced stop at $\pi/6$, feels down the arc to 2π. The hand feels down the arc to $3\pi/2$ and stops. The hand feels up the arc to π, unsettles the jar. The hand feels up the body, up the neck, knuckles the rim, all fingers down inside minus the thumb and stops. The hand feels down the other side of the jar, along the arc, two-thirds into Quadrant 2, forced stop at $3\pi/4$. The hand feels down the arc to π, unsettles the jar. The hand feels up the body, up the neck, knuckles the rim, down the neck, down the body, down the arc towards $3\pi/2$ and stops. The arm contracts, the hand comes back to the origin. The arm extends upwards, the hand inverts, comes to rest at $\pi/2$. The lid displaces to $\pi/4$ in Quadrant 1. The hand feels down the arc towards π. The hand unsettles the jar and stops. The hand feels up the arc towards $\pi/2$ and stops. The hand feels down the arc, nudges the lid at $\pi/4$. The hand grasps the lid. The hand drags the lid up the arc towards $\pi/2$, passes it, drags the lid down the arc until π, unsettles the jar, drops the lid. The hand grasps the lid, feels up the body with the thumb, up the neck, thumb and pinkie on rim, threads the lid on the neck. The hand twists the lid counterclockwise and nothing happens. The hand twists the lid clockwise and the mason jar seals. The arm extends upwards, the hand inverts, comes to a rest at the origin.

The Black Balloon

The garbage by the side of the complex rises waist-high; mostly shit stained t-shirts. I dig for the gold-foiled envelopes with a coat hanger. Easy to spot: gold on the outside, gold on the inside, especially in the sun, no clouds today: the foils shine thick. I collect nine or ten, lay them in the flat snow beside the garbage, step on and twist to clean them. Snow starts to fall from the sky: it meshes with the sun and nauseates. I wash my hands in the snow, pick up the envelopes and run left to the front door. I pass a tree. The only tree in the dirt yard. Skinny tree. On one of its lowest branches, a wrinkly, black balloon sways upside down, snagged. The ribbon tied to it shimmers foil gold in the sun snow. The ribbon unsnags and fits around my thumb snugly. I run to the front door, open the rusted outer door, then the inside door, make sure the balloon is inside, shut both, lock both. Inside, I wiggle off my shoes, walk down the hall, drop the foils by the stairs. My mom sits at the kitchen table, in front of the window, dark from the window behind: snow falls clear blue nausea. She smokes and stares at the ashtray, rubs the fallen ashes into a gauge on the table. The balloon skims lightly on the linoleum, in the light, the wrinkles cluster near the neck, top still tight: it statics dust. The power cuts off. She mouths something at me. I mouth something at her. She puts the cigarette in the ashtray, rises, mouths something else, walks over, nudges the balloon, kisses me on the head, rubs the back of my neck. She mouths something slowly, rubs her short hair, rubs her neck, walks back to her seat, takes another cigarette out of a pack, lights the new one, puts out the old one already in the tray. I turn and walk back to the stairs: the balloon follows on the ground, picking up more dust: thick, blue dust. I pick up the foils with my free hand and walk down the stairs in the faint light. At the bottom, I walk to the back door, littered with more foils: the light from the back door creases gold on the cement floor and walls. I bend down: the cement is cold on my hands and shins: the balloon rubs freely. The crawlspace by the back door blackens: the loose light from the window hinges on the wood rectangular frame. Cobwebs fray between the loose staples. As I crawl, the balloon bumps against the back of my leg. Two more wood rectangles pass. The power cuts back on. The lightbulb at the end of the crawlspace cuts on. Under the bulb, more scattered foils catch light, and reflect gold cracks on the concrete floor, walls and support columns. Two more wood rectangles pass and out into a low concrete square. My dad lies in the far right corner, under three patchwork blankets: his head raised on a pillow stuffed with plastic bags falling out the opening. He lifts his head: wrinkles at the neck: tight skin at his skull. My ribbon tied thumb swells with the weight of the crawl: I bunch the ribbon to the knuckle then wriggle it off: hold it now. The whole space stinks of shit. I tri-crawl over the foils, around his plates of powder and cups of water to his side. He mouths something. His cheekbones catch shadow: black flicks into his acne scars and whiskers: his eyes roll to the side and he looks at the balloon. I take the ribbon and wrap it around his finger poking up between two layers of blankets. He smiles: the teeth on his right side are gone. The balloon rolls around even though there's no breeze in the crawl space. I lift up the blanket and pull out the plate from under his ass: ripped t-shirt grease shit. I carefully rest the plate by the support column: the t-shirt slides a bit. I lift my hand and there's a sweat print on the cement. I hunch around and start organizing the foils into stacks of fifteen. Footsteps groan through the kitchen floorboards above. The power cuts out.

Still 1.21

Karms reads in his room, naked on an armchair draped in thin cobalt cotton, rubs his brow. On a table of cardboard rests a book: each page flickers stiff. A tall glass of white spills next to him: 1 sip per page. On 1 of the pages, my mother holds me. I remember everything about her. I remember nothing about her. I am her dress. She is half my face. She is roaring in my ear. Karms pauses the book and takes a sip.

Dust

The light seldom comes now. The light has been discussed. Light is a crutch. Dust floats down from the vents of the room. The dust is high-grade dust. It starts off low-grade and builds until it is high. It is most likely medium-grade all things balanced. Dust cannot be graded. As the chest gets slower, the dust gets thicker. As the dust gets thicker, it gets greyer. As the dust gets greyer, it gets bluer. As the dust gets bluer, it gets blacker. As the dust gets blacker, it gets blacker. Black mold. The kind behind every wall and lung. Black mold minus the mold. That color has been floating around in the skull for awhile. A discovery has happened. The dust is both lighter and denser than the air. The dust lightens at the top of the room, hovers erratically, then settles to the floor or on an angle or on a flat or semi-despondent surface. Dust logic appeals. Dust logic sticks. Dust logic accumulates. Dust logic piles. Dust logic heaps in its own logic. Dust logic is wiped eventfully. By rag. Rag logic. Rag logic wipes. Rag logic is the logic of They. They being Them to reiterate nauseously. They are all rags. Every last one of Them. They sicken me, back to the dust. Without the dust, there are no rags. Rags are dust, only dumb and dense. Rags are dust in denial. Rags are upsetting. Back to the dust. The dust accumulating in the room is both dry and moist. The dust sags down after a good pile. The composition of the dust remains unknown. The dust is not hair. They shaved the hair, one to two razors short, weeks ago. The skull hasn't been shaved in weeks. The dust might be hair. The dust is not skin. The skin was scrubbed weeks ago, one to two millimetres short, weeks ago. The dust might be skin. The dust might be hair, skin, other, all three together. The dust comes from outside the room. This fact inerts. The composition of the dust remains unknown. This is pleasing. The dust has piled during the conjecturing. The dust layer sags unevenly under its density. The pockets of depression are the bones of it. The dust covers the body, blanket and bed. The dust pacifies warm. The blinks shovel the dust from the open eyes. Two undusted ellipses slit the room. Two eyes in a large socket of black. The dust inches vertical. The dust inches warmth. The dust inches fur. The dust filters breath. The dust tastes of exhaust. Memory accumulates. The dust is memory. The dust is morning violet sky. On the street, behind a pink transformer, I wait for the rusted truck to stop in front. The truck idles: the four men, the bundle men, same size, same black stubble, same black hair, same overalls, step out, slam the door in unison, carry the same small bundles, same knot, disperse to different complexes, to toss the bundles down. I walk out from the transformer, behind the rust truck, bend down to the exhaust pipe, and suck the smoke, my first cigarette, into my throat, exhale, nothing, suck again, nothing. The men come back and laugh, tell me to fuck off, they laugh, all four leave a cigarette on the street, then step back in the truck and drive off. Misfire. Memory slows the brain. Back again to the dust. The dust has thickened. Superfine dust. The dust crackles and pops the longer it warms. Dust is breath. The dust is warm. The dust becomes intolerably warm. Venting is needed, yes, a vent. The left foot extends out of the dust, rotates, and retracts. The warm leaves. The dust is still intolerably warm. Venting is needed, yes, another vent is needed. The right foot extends out of the dust, rotates, and retracts. The dust becomes tolerably warm. The discomforts dissipate. Sleep can kick. The bladder ticks: on and off. The oscillation is what forces the urgency. If the bladder was empty or full, then the tick wouldn't happen. The dust would be continued undisturbed. The oscillation provides the sensation: sharp and dull: flex and relax. A piss has to transpire. Waiting happens. A hurt down in the tubes makes the heart grow fonder. Piss has nothing and everything to do with the heart. The piss might be a stone with alerter motives. The water is hard. Downstream from the mountains. Hard erodes off the rocks, into the water, into the mouth, into the kidney, into the tubes, into a stuck. Excitement would happen. Kidney dreams. The kidney pain is absent. No kidney dreams today. The tick still happens. The bed will be pissed if forced to. At this moment, the need for boredom outweighs the need for excitement. The piss will be stored away for a future convenience. Back to the dust. The dust accumulates more than description can provide. The blinks will not be used for shoveling. The dust is black. The dust is fur. Description can still be provided. The dust slickens between the fingers, thumb and index. The dust thickens over the face. The description is erroneous. Apologies thin. Erroneous at the bottom of it. The bottom of the skull is erroneous and what inhabits it. Little motion occurs in the black. Memory sludge: the cold of cold: sun minus the sun. At this depth, movement is reduced to conserve energy. The mind is dead skin: its arms are enlongated hair thin. The arms bend no more than 90 degrees and collapse. The float is initiated. The mind is both lighter and denser than the surrounding medium. The float is ideal. The mind drifts in the sludge. The mind siphons a memory more detritus than itself. Memory tastes black. Same shit different stratum. Erroneous and importance happens behind the eyes and the mouth of the mind. The dust domes up overhead.

Still 1.19

Winter's ditch spreads outside the City all cobalt. Ice tastes better when you suck it. A fence of chickenwire cages the banks: wind
iced hexagons. In the ditch, brown water staggers around the broken posts. A chain-link fence spreads a dam across the ditch 15 metres: the water eats past the chain-link: no dam after all. Only pill
bottles, plastic bags, wires, broken posts, stoves, wire fencing, ice,
circuit boards, trowels, tires, phone cords, door handles, cups, jars,
branches, razors, shirts, trunks, knives, power cables, playing cards,
coat hangers, ashtrays, doors, bowls, telephones, shoes, pots, candles,
oil, needles, pants, cardboard, hats, photographs, bed sheets, bottles,
blankets, wasp nests, doorframes, spoons, beds, freebase pipes, floorboards, yarn, towels, toilet seats, bath tubs, medical tubing, refrig-
erators, socks, wheelchairs, cigarette butts, knobs, dresses, buttons,
lightbulbs, drywall, balloons, transformers, birds, blankets, toilets,
Spades, bed frames, carpet, rope, asphalt, fluorescent tubes, yellow
paint, ladles, propane canisters, stove elements, tap heads, electrical
sockets, lamps, medical gauze dam. They dump every stone they find
into the ditch. They keep the round stones for themselves.

Window

Elliott wakes up, forty-five degrees against the wall, on the mattress. He stares at the window: he tightens his patchwork blanket: scraps of t-shirts, mangled letters, colors, numbers. He stands up on the mattress, rolls his toes, picks the sleep out of his eyes. His breath freezes. His patchwork blanket falls down, revealing another blanket, thin blue. His penis hangs free, then retracts inward. He calls Preeti two times. Silence. The blue light outside the window dims. Frost arcs on the pane: GONE scratched in the bottom curve of the arc. He walks to the edge of the mattress, closer to the window. His thin, blue blanket drops revealing a thinner, blue blanket. His leg and arm hair statics into the thin blanket. He steps off the mattress onto the wooden floorboards. His thinner blue blanket drops revealing a thinner, patchwork blanket: scraps of t-shirts, mangled letters, colors, numbers. He scratches the inside of his ear. He walks along a single floorboard to the window. At the window, he bends down, drops his blanket, revealing another thin blue one, and etches a? In the upper left of the window, the transformer hangs frosted over. He etches a frame on the window around the frosted transformer. His thin, blue blanket drops revealing another thin, blue blanket. He turns, walks over the same floorboard, back to the mattress, turns around. His blanket drops revealing his naked body. He picks up the thin, blue blanket and wraps it around his body and lies back down.

Still 1.16

A lightbulb, moon, sun or none of the above shines cobalt from the right onto the door, floor and wallpaper. Preeti drops her blue blanket: she shows her stretch marks on her hips and ass, rubs them up, then down, and up, then down, pale cracks of light. Talking is absent. She drops her blue blanket. She braces her wrist on the chair back, dreads down her back, squats, shoves a cup the size of 4 cups under and pisses. She gets up, wipes with her blanket, the chair falls forward, dents the doorframe. Stretch marks under her eyes. She leaves.

Dome

Dead dust. The air is dust. The temperature is dust. The bed is dust. 360 degrees of dust ground up half a metre. Breathing is the sound. Faint rectangles appear above. Some rectangles more curved than others. The rectangles lighten from black to blue to grey. The number of rectangles are easily forgotten. The sound of my skull on the pillow distracts. The rectangles lighten grey from blue around the edges and inward. The lighter the rectangles become, the more slurring occurs. The slurring comes from outside the rectangles. The slurring becomes voices. The slurring is now voices. Scratching starts too. The voices are now scratching. The scratching becomes frequent. From this angle, the voices scratch at the rectangles. This is probably incorrect. A chunk of rectangle from the top right falls from above. Smaller chunks follow the chunk. Powder follows the smaller chunks. Finer powder follows the powder. The finer powder tastes of exhaust. In the centre above, a light blue circle appears. The voices become stronger. A hole breaks, a long hole, more powder, white powder, snow, light falls in, as it always does, and blinds, as it always does. White fingers poke through. Multiple fingers enter. The fingers are stacked with gold rings. The reflection is white as all reflected light appears. Rings cover every centimetre of the fingers. Chunks fall indiscriminately. The fingers become hands. The hole becomes larger and more light. The hands rotate circular, clockwise and counterclockwise. The hands latch and peel the rectangles outward, making a sound I've never heard. The chunks and powder continues to fall. Faces appear: freckles, bleeding lips and teeth, ungapped and perfect. "Found you," they say, all in unison. They are children. The children wrinkle deep in themselves. Unfamiliar children: wrinkles, freckles, liverspotted, bleeding lips, teeth, ungapped and perfect, blond or white hair. I don't know their names, but I'm sure they suit them. The light, the opening, no dust, but light. The children watch overhead for minutes. The light dims and the faces pull away. A door slides shut. A good silence falls. I nub my face out of the hole. The room is calm and cold.

Food 1.4

Four hands stacked, four hands fat holds a clear bowl in front of my face. The ladle drops a dollop of melted Vaseline, ripples up the curves, loosens steam. The he says nothing. The ladle pulls up. Above, a hand cracks a white packet of white salt in the middle of the bowl, ripples the surface. The hand cracked packet pulls up. A half-sphere of black in the middle. Clear gel still circles on the outside. The other he says nothing. Black rectangles flutter down, some stick to the sides of the bowl and clot. Another he coughs. Some rectangles ripple the liquid and spider black to the bottom of the bowl. The she says nothing. Her fingers, powdered black, grid the surface and clot. She lifts up her left hand and covers her eyes, bends her head, and spits. All four people slowly back up and out the room. The bowl wobbles on my chest.

Still 1.04

St. Nowhere: a place, all things inside, all things cobalt, inside the afternoon. The Spade sleeps on the nightstand, pulsing brass and glass. A nulled pictureframe above the bed. A pictureframe empties quicker when you use it. Walls scuffed cobalt: cracks along every one. The brass bed frame arcs splinterful. A blue, thin blanket gifted to me by someone who's dead and gone. The blanket will be recycled: lost and found. A pillow slinks against the bed frame. I am thinking. They are coming again. Premonitions are a bitch. They being them, to reiterate dimly. They have already come. They are giving me a few minutes to collect my thoughts. A few minutes collect nothing. They are outside with a gurney, a superfine gurney. They didn't mention where they are taking me. They didn't mention anything about a cure. This pleases me. I reflect on my time here: done. I lay on the edge of the bed because it is the calmest. The last moment or 2 or 3 or more cracks. A reach is made backward. The arms are unfolded. The sheets are messed impartially. Sheets are made to be messed. The piss of future convenience begins. You want Them to think. You don't want Them to think you tidied for Them. That would be rolling over for Them, playing nice and skinny for Them, 1 more needle in the hay with Them, that would be the final sign They've destroyed your mental decorum, that would be Them fucking you, then you watching your decorum leak out. You don't want them to think you've saved them any time. The piss ends. A superfine piss. The sheets are best messed: anger leaks into every layer. The door slides open. The gurney peeks in.

Obsequence

queue, hallway straight down maybe a curve down further, too dark or curvy to tell, lights turn on still down the queue increasingly and hang still above from the ceiling where else with cables what else lights turn on ahead at no unpredictable intervals, queue straightens down no curves this now established, 100 metres red diode numbers display box 1 by 0.2 metres numbers eat themselves out left-to-right, red-to-black across the box, 100 metres is known because it's above, 1 metre above, numbers and letters eat across the box established, thoughts into spade still part of thoughts, spade affect, no, stupid, nothing can't affect nothing, spade loads on the chest, clear box stuffed with everything thought seen ate shit fucked etc., spade nulled and filled, then nulled and filled, more could have been stuffed into spade, no, thoughts are no longer available or other, attempts will be made but no broken promises either, 100 metres above, numbers eat above across in the dark intentional in the most premeditated, that is premeditated, in front in the queue, a skull rises up on its pillow, a sphere and a metal band and prickles of hair, skull tilts to the left and down, first movement in this temperature-controlled space, the queue to orientate, this is important in some circles, silence breaks at the back in the queue behind, the new skull, forward skull for the sake of orientation, 2 metres ahead exact because the box above it eats

98 metres left-to-right, red-to-black, 100 minus 98 is 2 metres, know that math, they can't keep that one away, they being them, to reiterate dimly, they will no longer be distinguished, they're not hiding this one, the numbers that is, they never tried to hide this one, they don't not care but really care in the worst way, doesn't matter anymore, never really did,

jerk, sudden, no, push, pull, sudden, no, forward, nausea, no, too much, was really, skull clichéd to the pillow as all skulls are paper clichéd, conjecture, vague apology, front skull still in front still with a little inertia settles, still no face no forehead, no, a little forehead a little face right temple angled bone, prickles of hair short as conjecture same color as conjecture, all skulls shade the same shaved texture, just one skull forward, forward skull, a good skull to look at, a superfine skull, above forward skull the box 96 metres eats itself left-to-right, red-to-black, the box directly above eats 98 metres, jerk forward in jerks of 2 metres, 2 metres per time seconds minutes, 2 metres per jerk, rates are too vague to attain at this point comeback to later maybe if there's time, no, no time, 2 metres per can't tell, leave it at that, numbers man's best thing, leaving it, each side of the gurney, on a gurney or what seems like a gurney because all words are gurneys all more piss shit stained than others, conjecture, vague apologies the most concrete kind, the gurney should have been mentioned before, this detail should have been mentioned before, details lack ideal placement anyway, the gurney may have been mentioned, dark above both sides of the gurney parallel nothing each side dark dry stink of bleach, the eyes fail losing sight in the right and left more so than in the right, the blinks clean little, a blink wets better without purpose, when the blink happens it only sharpens the dark on each side of the gurney, walls of glass or plastic, no, glass for sure, glass cubes or might be plastic or other, no, walls reflect cold blunt glass enough for light to pass to illuminate more dark inside the cubes and the more dark inside that dark and the more dark inside that dark, same cubes parallel down the queue, some cubes lighten too far down too far down the queue for a verification, eyes focus to the point of unfocused, blinking is moisture, blinking is needed, the eyes get more useless and sore at a constant rate, dry air and temperature aid in the worst way, moisture not coming, they, they being them, to reiterate vaguely, vague is as vague does, they've thought of everything, they have giant warehouses where they dehydrate monkeys or some other reasonable simian shaved skulls in a mini-queue sided by mini-cubes on mini-gurneys with mini-spades under mini-boxes with mini-diodes that eat numbers left-to-right, red-to-black, then mini-jerks, then mini-confusions, then mini-conjectures, then mini-vague apologies, no more innerspace monkeys, a blink is needed, no more monkeys or some other reasonable conjecture here or else where blinked out already lucky,

jerk, sudden, push, pull, push, yes, sudden, forward, now, 96 metres, above, now, no nausea, no, a blink full of nausea then gone acclimatized to the jerks, now the fluid of wait settles tasting of plaque, conjecture, vague apology, the skulls are queued but how many, calculate the skulls, yes, counting skulls is a good calculation, assume 100 metres at start, then the jerk forward 2 metres per can't tell 50 skulls in the queue plus more every jerk maybe 50 skulls for sure then 50 gurneys plus more maybe every jerk 50 gurneys sure then 50 boxes overhead plus more, no, no more every jerk maybe then 50 glass cubes no more each jerk maybe most lit worse than others,

jerk, sudden, sudden, push, sudden, push, forward, now, 94 metres above, blunt air in front of skull not forward skull but my skull should have clarified, sleep is needed used now, numbers found the skulls gurneys boxes cubes, sleep can start now, sleep or some other reasonable substitute, but, what, wait, the queue might elongate, queue started at 100 metres surely 100 metres unsure, it was, no, doesn't matter in the end, if there's an end, won't, can't matter, a meal, a last

189

meal needed but unlikely, a last meal possibly already, they've already provided sustenance in the purest uncut powders carbohydrates protein vitamins trace minerals and others some missing naturally, something that resembles care has been provided, more water was needed, the amount given usually bordered on no water, lukewarm to luker warm, the lack of water produces shit stones, a bitch to get out, the anus sucks thoroughly then haphazardly then the drop, cycle of the bowels, conjecture, vague apology, medication has been provided, uncut powders too pressed into compact but often jagged uneasily swallowable pills, at the end the cure might be provided, the cure given, no, doesn't exist, might, no, might, no, they might change their mind, no, their piece of mind, the size of the hole in the arm before the IV slips in, that one slipped out, conjecture, vague apology, they don't plus pieces of mind away only minus, no change of mind is possible, don't know that, don't want to know that, not my fault or any other skulls forward or maybe back,

jerk, sudden, not so, sudden, forward, 92 metres above, sleep is needed, yawn happens, sleep stuck between the teeth, conjecture, vague apology, familiar, sleep may have passed already, a black calm may have been missed, all calms are black, can't be sure, attempts are made familiar,

jerk, sudden, very, 90 metres, above, 10 metres from the assumed start, the arm untucks out the blanket, doesn't matter which one, 50/50 chance guess the right, why not, no, the left, the cotton sheet offers no resistance, the arm dangles catches nothing, half-expected floor from the distance of the box to my skull, assumed lower, the arm dangles, the arm rubs nothing, done, the arm comes back up and under the sheet, enough for now, a thrill skullfuckingly thrill, pardon my skull,

jerk, there it goes, getting the hang of the push now, 88 metres above, the metres flush, metres are blisters, conjectures, vague apology, a

body walks from the dark forward on the right from a distance un-
specified, hearing is still possible because there are still ears, no seeing, eyes not working it's their fault, steps uneven with a drag or panting is possible or parting breath from one of the other skulls if there's
other skulls besides front skull, steps getting firmer, a face crosses, a
three-pronged face passes, steps getting blunt over the right shoulder,
back, gone,

surprise, again, the jerk, push or, no, no push, someone would have
to be in front hunched or unhunched over obstructing the view of
forward skull, pushes are gifted all the time, doubtful here, thoughts
can push on anyone in the eyes, 86 metres are good metres not 100
not 0 off the middle somewhere, 100 metres hours ago not sure can't
hours or minutes, hard to tell when the legs don't stir or anything else
for that matter, the testis and the penis each shrivel in their own logic
can't be plumped now stasis that back to the arms already enough after the dangle, been said took the shit out of me, all action is shades of
fingernail, fingernails are shade, all action shades, conjectures, vague
apology, alley shade, a last alley stroll would be good, one final time,
why final, just a stroll, not this stroll, a shit stroll this is, no, a queue of
my own, a queue of my own is needed,

jerk, 84 metres above, lips function seamlessly, offtrack, where was,
yes, the alley and the stroll, the last stroll in the moon or sun or bulbs
and gravel sharp getting sharper, only sharp gravel survives each step
left then right then repeat accordingly left and right death rattle the
ankles, only one stroll, one stroll up the alley, until a nice piece of
sheet metal is found to crawl under or a nice right angle to clamp
onto, get a space alone then wait,

jerk, 82 metres above, quick one, quick jerk, now if all were that quick
it would be a conveyer, a shitty conveyer, no, but it's a gurney they
put me on after vague, what was before the gurney being put on the

gurney, scratch that null that, a space white, angled sheet filled dis-
ordered, skull runnelled, the dig will happen later, dig around for it
later, when there's a later, if there's a later, no later will be later, space
was only metres ago, 82 above, 18 metres ago then the jerk started, the
dark rolling jerking,

jerk, 80 metres above, convenient, 18 metres from the start of the
queue the space the sheets, no, 100 minus, no, 20 metres ago but there
should be more distance, from the space to the start of the queue
noisy space as noiseless as a push not a jerk then a lift somewhere and
then a turn definitely a turn then the queue can't figure must be 20
metres for sure from the space of can't, skull can't remember like it
used to, another one, another insight will stagger along shortly, here
comes one right now, not mental but this time but another real, the
steps come from behind and right, the steps start at the back work
their way up more frequent now sharper above than before stop,
hinges flush, the steps don't pass, the steps stuck in the back behind
the skull, vague apology for causing excitement,

jerk, one of many, queued dark hallway, force mass acceleration then
transformer then death then exit point then the stink, conjecture,
vague apology, getting over the skull with that one, dim back down,
78 metres above, a quick blink, a fine blink premeditated in the fullest, best one so far, forward skull still in front on pillow, hallway left
hallway right left cubes right cubes dark same temperature, consistency must be kept, the paste of consistency in the mouth where it
belongs, the paste cakes up back up the skull leaks back down half-up
then straight ahead, conjecture, vague apology, spade still here hasn't
left yet or showing signs of

jerk, 76 metres above, that jerk took the shit out of me, where was, spade
not hurting anyone affectionate as a wandering inanimate box can be,
skin clear, no, the spade has no skin shifts dark and back gone and back

jerk, 74 metres above, jerk so close to the last one, where, yes, spade, if breathe was still possible it would be directed at it, fingerprints would then be applied if the fingers were still working and the ambient air temperature would allow, small-to-medium fingerprints for the eyes, a finger drag for a smile, breath wouldn't last long on its skin, no, not skin that's anthropomorphism dirty good to the fullest, spade's skin is made of guesses, black and white guesses, a blow is attempted from the mouth, attempts are fragile, trachea not in the upright position, a smile is attempted but the breath hasn't made it far enough, trachea not in the upright position hasn't been for metres, a neutral tap is given on its guesses already established, the tap, the neutral tap, the tap statics a thumbprint, memory statics, memory ashes, conjecture, vague apology, ash prints, five fingers, palm absent on the wall of a familiar forgotten room, all rooms are forgotten, preeti, ash hands, preeti, ash hands, her fingers tip black, grey down the gradient to the knuckles, her fingers root in ashes, roaches, ash roaches in the ashtrays, ash roaches for a suitable use at a future need, no roaches found, only ash, only ash is ascertained, memory ashes, conjecture, vague apology,

jerk, again, sudden, so, not, so sudden, spade sits like a good box on the chest, 72 metres above, spade closest pet had here, there were other pets ago buried ago, locations buried too, must wallow in con-jecture, closest thing to a pet had here or outside can't remember where the others the pets were buried, mice fat or skinny border-ing on rat or they were rats, no, no rats just mice fat or skinny mice all died, r-selected, all species are r-selected now, this knowledge is attained how, there was the first, white one, size of a pill bottle, daymare name was thought so clever, died, buried it in three old, plastic bags, dug hole under the cement tiles in the alley next to the raspberry bush with the turpentine berries, then chug-a-lug, stupid name, thirsty little face black, died, found belly-up in the corner of its cage then tossed in the dumpster or was it daymare don't know anymore, ice tiles holes all wrong, no matter there were others, can't all be remembered,

jerk, sudden, sudden, over, the overstimulation then the bore, the IV then the hole, conjecture, vague apology, 70 metres above, closer never gets closer, still dark metres only change, the ceiling first occurs blurs well, eyes worsening distinctly, no distinct shades of worse because all shades are worse, the ceiling is nothing to think complex about, some grey pink bumps, various fist-sized lumps solid splatter hucked up plaster pulp fiberglass, someone must have hucked solid, the arms plastered cracked mud skin dust on the elbows wherever a bend breaks dust on finger joints too, hucking shit up at the ceiling hoping the shit will settle, huck and hope, huck and hope repeat and repeat after hour and day after day and night after night,

month after month conjecture after conjecture until finished, a job done quite greasily, they being them, to reiterate vaguely, they must have got someone to huck solid until both arms dislocated into darkness,

66 meter above, 0 is 66 metres down, 2 metres ago, 68 metres above, 4 metres ago, 70 metres away, could count back to 100, 100 metres back to the space and the doctor, a doctor was there too, vague apology, another detail forgotten him already forgotten name already just a name now already feel better minded already,

jerk, 72, no, 64 metres above good number plenty of metres, a final pleasure is needed, a quick pleasure then back to the count, skull strong body string, conjecture, vague apology, the body best equals still, the rub can't get going trying blinking, no blinking, eyes closed trying little-to-no response wiggle from side-to-side in the skull in hopelessness of friction rub together memories of genitals encountered gently or not, friction makes heart grow fonder, no, too little

194

friction in the skull, hardness cannot be acquired, the memory sta-
sises, front skull or the bodies passing infrequently might view the act
in process of ensuing,

jerk, 62 metres above, accidental meeting of mental and physical,
no doubt something or someone would watch but what of the other
skulls, another skull in the queue, not calculated rubbed thoroughly,
a deeper calculation is needed, not front skull in front too dignified
beautiful, blindspotted skull, knowledge can be gained from someone's skull, a well-positioned skull, a silent skull, a screaming skull,
no, knowledge cannot be gained in that manner,

jerk, 60 metres above, forward skull can it for neutrality see behind
might be able to turn its head don't think it would catch or watch for
reasons too blindspotted, but, wait, front skull must have a skull in
front, a fronter skull, this fronter skull must have a still fronter skull
in front of it, conversely there must be a skull behind me, behind
skull for consistency and a behinder skull behind it and so on, 50/50
chance of behind skull,

behind skull has to be, one at front another at back symmetry of
skulls mine a part of the middle, yes, maybe 25, no, 20, no, 21 skulls
back maybe 25, no, 29 skulls forward skull ended by skulls, if there
is a skull at the back of my own is it watching in the most asocial
of social space, friction should be deployed for old time's sake, one
last friction, disgust is friction, desire is dead, skull runnelled with
it, conjecture, vague apology, if behind skull watches from behind
the palms deep in rub, it would have to see over my skull, old lumpy
empty might block its eyes, disgust might be elicited, desire might
be elicited, desire is dead dead we all fall down, its eyes not skull far
enough up the pillow bored breath on my neck, conjecture, vague
apology, a poor-to-fair seat is not possible, no proper elevation and
therefore arousal lacks,

jerk, two pillows are needed for proper elevation, two pillows accidently given while all other skulls or not possibly only get one, a mistake is possible, no, maybe, no, at most not, they, they being them, to reiterate nauseously, wouldn't fuck up, they treat all perfectly marginally equally if less, even if behind skull was accidentally gifted with two pillows it couldn't, maybe, view,

jerk, 56 metres above, behind skull might can't watch, behind skull might watch, no matter the merrier, respect queue decorum enough to break it, boredom maintains it, a break in queue decorum proves necessary, boredom maintains it, just because they treat us biotically and abiotically simultaneously, no, somewhere in the middle, no, off the middle, don't know what that means, doesn't mean that two pillows offer necessarily a greater angle of vision, the neck needs more vertical but that would cause pain and pain would cause boredom and boredom would cause sleep in the skull, behind skull the skull in question, behind skull would be asleep skull, the spade might be on its chest if it has one, an assumption is made, however the spade could be tucked in tight elsewhere on the left, right, front, back, under gurney, spades are tricky that way,

if a spade was on its chest a further obstacle would be provided, an attempt could be made, even if behind skull witnesses the act, no matter the merrier, an attempt could be made, one last friction, one last memory hard on the gurney, if a dying skull performs in a queue and its body can't perform has anything happened been asserted, the question fails, the question falls to shit, shit falls, shit asserted, conjecture, vague apology,

jerk, 52 metres above, words are embers in the firebarrel awaiting piss, embers are dirt in denial, words ember then sizzle then cake then dirt then conjecture, vague apology, blinks cannot happen, erection cannot happen, memory cannot happen, an idea about an idea, meta-friction, a light turns on ahead on the left in one of the cubes, all the skull talk dulled the queue, stunk it up slow, no, no apologies, the light remains on up ahead 2 or 3 no 4 jerks ahead,

jerk, 50 metres above, middles are halfway deads, only 50 metres ago was the start of the queue because it was 50 metres ago, long distance ago same dark hallway now as the start with some interest coming on the left in one of the cubes medium cube, no, all cubes the same size, medium thin, no, thick pale blue glass maybe plastic no scuffs scrapes, don't imagine in the queue much fighting falling tipping happens, a tip over is needed, if the body cooperated, inertia is need-ed, left-to-right then right-to-left, repeated over a period of seconds minutes left-to-right then right-to-left repeat until the right never right time then the tip then on the floor blankets corded around the legs and gurney roll for a corner, no corners are visible only a straight hallway, straight queue, problems are encountered, dead could be played where floor meets glass right angle for hiding, stillness could be played, breath could be held, dead could be played, they wouldn't notice too dark stagnant, even with the dark, even with the shit eyes, a crawl could be made, a crawl back to the start, a crawl back 50 me-tres to what, the worst could happen, a complementary lift back on the gurney gifted, no, the queue would be bunged, a complementary lift back to the start of the queue gifted, the queue starts over again, a complementary flop into a gravel pit gifted, no, a nice pit is uncertain now, the queue's surroundings are unknown, they would toss me out, a hole of my own would have to be found, a hole of one's own, a good hole can't be promised anymore, a hole is a hole is a hole, no, the tip is irrelevant, the mess would be cleaned, the me would be cleaned, the ankles would be rattled, the veins would be slapped, a hole can be dug here, back on track towards 0, why 0 why 0 is 0 the end, 0 is a good number, hope cannot be spelt without the 0,

jerk, 48 metres above, halfway a little less now still too early in the process of enjoying the last jerk when jerked away, the light is closer, the cube is closer, the cube was forgotten, no, well, briefly, the cube, the surprise, one more jerk should suffice then wait for the interest, no, the skull will be turned away to the right, interest will be compounded, interest will be knotted, the interest will be doubled, the threshold of boredom will be killed twice, the science of surprise stinks of bleach, inexact as insects, conjecture, vague apology, the skull faces right to the wall of black cubes in waiting,

jerk, the neck's numb knot ruins the surprise, surprises are meant to be ruined, in the cube through the pale blue glass two fluorescent tubes graft in the ceiling horizontal no buzzing because of the glass no flickering clean above two rows or three or maybe more of people doctors or others smocks pale blue standard slippers pale blue some smocks more tied than others cords strings dangle from the backs more than others some ass cracks more visible than others some hairier than others some sweatier than others some dryer than others all have hats those hats don't know the name of pulled tight those ones blue cotton layered plastic on the underside to encourage sweat, all watch a screen on the wall slight tear bottom right curling down then coiling upwards inwards unimportant, on the screen a body projected a body on a gurney face fallen as all faces get looking toward the left nothing but skull fine skull lumps buried under shaved hair a spade on its chest white and black floods across it, above the body another window or screen with two rows or three or maybe more of people pixilated smocks slippers some smocks slippers more pixilated some ass cracks more pixilated than others pixilated hats all watch a pixilated rectangle on the wall of white no black maybe, the skull on the screens appears familiar, all skulls appear familiar, this skull is more familiar than familiar, conjectures are made,

jerk, 46 metres, light diffuses through the back left into the glass of the next cube, light does the darndest things, the neck will not be twisted for a better view, the eyes adjust themselves, front skull still there still snug, the act to be committed is forgotten, no, the act, the rub,

jerk, the rub, the memory hard on the gurney, one or two memories from under the sheets for some reason, under the sheets no friction anymore, the air of dignity has to be dug away, my own hole has to be dug, no one else will because no one else can,

jerk, 42 metres above, numbers are meant to be counted, the numbers are counted, why, just count forward, what else to do, while still stay still, skull strong body string, conjecture, vague apology, more cannot be pictured, in time maybe 50 metres, don't want to get interests up now,

jerk, 40 metres now, a hard thought remains absent, wait, no, even if front skull tilted now tired now almost a forehead my first forehead in the queue, no, my second forehead, a forehead maybe more, walked by earlier, that forehead was too brief, that forehead is inapplicable, this forehead borders on meaningful, another light forward on the left turns on in the pale blue glass another surprise, the another surprise turns off, the surprise is ruined before the ruin, a quick ruin nevertheless, a memory should be thought, a memory, a shiny, a shiny one, one shiny memory to make it all shiny, not like the mice, a shit memory that one was, a memory no premeditation, maybe like rails on the gurney or cube lights or the lights above, shiny, get shiny at a queue like this, how does one get shiny, a memory shines how,

jerk, 40 metres above, no 38 metres above, an error, wouldn't want to error the count now for some reason deeper than my skull will let me, self-awareness is an itch lashed on lymph wide aerosol deep, conjecture, vague apology, not shiny enough, a trigger is needed, a shiny trigger in the queue, nothing reflects, yet, no, the cure, a cure for the trigger, no, no sure trigger, no sure cure, deadend, not even a u-turn at the end of queue, no, conjecture, vague apology, no, nothing at the end, most likely nor anything after, no, don't know that, that surprise, that final surprise, the death surprise, that surprise might be a ruin or a ruined ruin, that surprise is nothing like their surprise, they being them's surprise, they can't know anything of that surprise, that surprise only happens in the skull and deeper wandered, even if the cure happens at the end, what is to be felt, what is to be done, where is to be went, who is to be felt, all ends in shades of queue, virus x, cancer y, death z, all same queue, all end same queue,

preeti, red, others went seconds, minutes, days, months, years, no, not days or months maybe months ago, what happened together at the end will never be known, preeti, red, it was just days it was just nights, both were wasted equally, we were nothing, nothing is something, born with nothing then more nothing then less nothing then lesser nothing in the end, that's something,

jerk, 34 metres above, good number for no reason, a light, one or two or three or four jerks ahead turns on in a cube, inside will be interest to starve off the fat of boredom fat exactly that plenty of that to go around the skull, conjecture, vague apology, the light in the cube turns off, a ruin, story of the queue, epiphanies are needed, meninges of epiphanies, conjecture, no apology, preeti, red, thoughts of people, acts committed in private or pubic, acts in trees days spent, no, no trees, all dead, all gone dead, shit dust days in the skull nothing just dark and skulls pillows maybe foreheads lights boxes cubes frequent forward motion and a count, conjectures, vague apologies, a light on, the left turns on one jerk away, a surprise unexpected, the bowels tick, the sphincter of surprise dilates,

the count is ignored, plastic count warm dull, the surprise ruins, the cube is well-lit, two rows or three or four not four of people may have seen prior metres ago sit on benches pale blue smocks hats same ones as prior same shades of asses as prior, a television set at front, a medium-to-large television set plays a hill green perfect middle medium-to-large size as hills go grass and sky blue and green, the heads vibrate marginally right and left, repeat, they sit and watch the television, a hill how cozy, a hill shaved of buildings, a ditch crawls in, a fine ditch and a mailbox, a boy or adult, no, a boy walks to the box kicks it starts picking up grass, no, rocks traps them down the rust gullet slow and fast, the boy appears familiar, the ditch appears familiar, all boys and ditches are familiar, the boy and the ditch are more familiar than familiar, more conjectures are made, the people in the cube lose interest, interest is lost, 30 metres are still available, this surprise stinks, another whiff of surprise is possible

jerk, more watching was needed, no, bored better off with the jerks, still more 30 metres to watch, lips parch together, body bloats tight, the eyes need to seal, fluids must be conserved, the eyes' seals might have to be broken again, fingers arms legs are swollen with energy, seals are meant to be broken,

jerk, queue is now heating lukewarm to luker warm, right range for growth, no more numbers, numbers make sickness, numbers are dull and humidity controlled, thoughts skull sweat, 100 metres is missed, three digits are brief, two digits are lonely, one digit is still, this insight lacks, 100 metres is not missed

jerk, front skull still same pillow angle, front skull angles the same but lower than the previous low, 26 now, 26 metres, the seal is broken, the seal was never sealed completely, fluids are meant to leak, now, leakage is important because all observations in the queue have been so stable routine controlled, the queue is being savoured, this is your singularity and its getting infinitely singular one irrelevant quanta of violence at a time, done, the savouring is done, bored still, nothing said, nothing moved silenced, vents leak silence, conjecture, vague apology, the silence cannot be broken because it was broken at the beginning of the queue, the spade is gone off the chest, the spade crawled (or whatever) away in the heat of boredom, the spade cannot be blamed, the spade is hiding between the legs neck pillow knees gurney under gurney most likely not, gone,

jerk, 24 metres, front skull still, a memory is needed still, a memory, one memory, one shiny one, one memory at the most, two at the most, no, one memory will do, one memory to turn the trick, one will do but maybe, no, the one might not turn, a second memory is needed for a reserve, the second might not reflect any better, a third memory is needed, no, the memories are unnaturally plural, desire does the darndest things,

jerk, 22 now, good metres, the jerks are needed to disintact the skull, the jerks starve the boredom, back to the two memories, the neurons need restriction, leakage is to be kept to a minimum, now the choice of neurons, don't want leakage already enough of that, a spade full of that, shit siphon, a gentle choice is needed, a forceful choice might force memory back out the skull, memory onto pillow, memory down spine, memory pool by the asshole, memory pool by the pis-shole, conjectures, vague apology,

jerk, the numbers will no longer be counted, a new distraction is needed to erect one memory, two memories at the most, no, one memory for sure, two memories are more than needed, the second might bung up the first, the first might amplify the second, the second might bung up the first, already mentioned, the first may fist the second, the second might amplify the first, both or one might botch itself, one runt exists out of the two memories maybe, there has been one or two precome mice, turpentine, and adjectives but not enough good warm relief, the skull fevers, the rub resumes, nothing comes up nothing white space some flicks of black, one more rub is needed, one more trick is needed to turn, a light turns on the right side, a cube, the rubbing halts, a new surprise, the position will get better with jerks, two jerks ahead, no, one jerk, the cube clears violet, so close yet so close, one jerk of the gurney is needed,

jerk, the neck is meant to be cracked, the walls of the cube oscillate white and violet, an old man rests on a table, old man eyes blunt upwards one leg one arm chest stiff white hair full white ventilator faced half gasmask to the eye bags under the eye holes, a tube from the wall, a tube of striated metal vents gas air nutrients perhaps all down into the face holes, perhapses pump into the face holes, the lower ones, nothing vents out, perhapses siphon back up, his head falls faces the glass, full skull of white hair with a blot of anger, two eyes one large white another larger white, wrinkles fan out from the eye bags over cheeks over brow shallow wrinkles, the chest stiffens with perhapses, falls with perhapses, the perhapses stop stiffening and falling,

jerk, 14 metres above, the numbers will not be mentioned again, 14 metres, 14 whole metres, a memory is still needed, one memory or two, no, one memory is still needed, two memories have proven unsustainable

jerk, 12 metres, overhead now, further cubes of light are unlikely, above behind the number boxes a screen blurs, a screen bright far ahead, a screen 3 metres by 3 metres, over the boxes, a triangle of light halfway up the screen, another triangle of light on top, on that triangle, another triangle of light on top of that triangle, assume it will be impotent, the screen should have been mentioned earlier, details leak never at the right time, front skull still there in front, behind skull maybe

jerk, 10 metres, 10 whole metres, the metres will not be counted anymore, five jerks, one does not need to be carried, gratuitous almost over, there is nothing else to think, 10 metres, 10 whole metres, no five, five jerks, dildoing

jerk, last metres of thought unlikely, the spade still hides somewhere on the gurney, sign of intelligence, intelligent machine, more understanding is needed, no, back to the metres and the screen, the figures will be able to be identified soon in one jerk or two

jerk, a large screen blurs behind the boxes, the screen is 6 metres by 6 metres, gurneys boxes skulls shaved some more upright than others triangle forward into the dark into the center, another large screen above the skulls 1 metre by 1 metre line of beds gurneys skulls shaved some more pixilated than others triangles forward into above center, a large pixel 0.5 metre by 0.5 metre line of pixels some more pixilated than others triangles forward into white and black,

the numbers will not be related, the numbers cannot be endured, the numbers can be endured because there is little else, one memory is needed, no memories are available, all going gone, no memories, no one memory, just 0, better all better, skull better

jerk, front skull disappears under shredded black tires, preeti, the neck cracks, above the screen above amplifies picture accordingly, description is longer needed, the skulls on-screen vanish point back, the skulls on-screen vanish point vertical, the triangles become one, the points become more pointed, the points pixilate together in unison, conjectures accumulate, the skulls are art here, the art of they's art, all art here, enjoyment, they's art, enjoyment, no conjecture, no vague apology, they, they being them, to put it dimly, they will deplete the skulls, they will deplete themselves, then the final theys will snap their own necks sucking their own cocks cunts whatever, no conjecture, no apology, then out, this reality is a shit hole, no conjecture, no apology ever, out forever out

Resolutions: o.

Hopes: o.

Memory: o.

Meter: o.

Obsequins

Winter, violet night, light pollution cracks the clouds serrated. Snow statics across the garbage, trees, fence. Outside, the snow sickles on the bottom-right corner of the window. In the kitchen, my father sits at the table backlit by pale violet, I sit on a chair across from him, my feet on his knees. He cuts my toenails with a small knife, handle black, plastic gnarled. The lightbulb overhead flickers off and on. He pauses when the light flickers off. He cuts three times per nail, right-to-centre, centre blunt short, end of centre to the left edge as close as he can to the skin, each nail a stumped hexagon. I run the tips of my fingers over the tri-blunt nails on my left foot. After every cut he twists off the nail up and tears to ensure an edge for the next cut. He drops the cut nail into a gauge in the table. The vents are silenced. I hold my left foot for warmth, try to stitch all ten fingers between the five toes. My father's pale breath warms my right foot. On the table rests a large test tube. A white serrated cap rests besides a sharpening stone. He finishes cutting the right foot, my fingers stitch into it. He checks his thigh for any missed nails. He reaches over, picks up the test tube, unscrews the cap. He rubs out the nails from the gauge, pinches them up and tries to drop them into the mouth of the tube. Some nails fall back on the table, he dabs them up and in. He hands me the tube, I slide off the chair and walk to the sink, lift the faucet.

No water drips down. He lights a cigarette and points to a mason jar half-filled with water besides the sink. He takes a drag, rises, walks to the sink, unscrews the jar. I hand him the tube, he ashes in it then pours water in the narrow mouth of the tube with his fist funnelled. He screws on the cap tight, shakes the water off his hand onto the floor, ashes in the sink, sits back down, legs crossed looking out the window. I shake the tube holding it up to the light. Each nail a black silver of sun: ash and nails and bubbles up round the edges to the glass curve cakes, then fall float and fall, bubble down and settle. The light flickers off.

LITERARY SOURCES:

Alden, W.L. "The Purple Death". *Cassell's Family Magazine*. London, 1895.

Conrad, Joseph. *Heart of Darkness*. Ed. D.C.R.A. Goonetilleke. Toronto: Broadview, 2002.

Derrida, Jacques. *The Gift of Death*. 2nd ed. Trans. David Willis. Chicago: Chicago UP, 2008.

Internet, The.

Kharms, Daniil. "Blue Notebook #10". *Today I Wrote Nothing: The Selected Writings of Daniil Kharms*. Trans. Matvei Yankelevich. New York: Overlook Duckworth, 2007.

Seneca. "Phaedra". *Four Tragedies and Octavia*. Trans. E.F Watling. New York: Penguin, 1966.

"Transcript of President Bush's address to a joint session of Congress on Thursday night, September 20, 2001". *Whitehouse.gov*. 26 October 2008.

ACKNOWLEDGEMENTS

I would like to thank first and foremost Robert Majzels for his friend-
ship and all of the knowledge, conversations, and perspectives shared.
Without you this book would not be possible. Thanks also to Claire
Hout and Ugo.

I would also like to thank Suzette Mayr for her friendship and the
early eyes on the project.

Many thanks to Tasnuva Hayden, my editor in words and life.

Thanks to Fraser Wright for his pen work. See you in the office.

Much gratitude to the Social Sciences and Humanities Research
Council for the support and the time to write.

Thank you to Jay MillAr, Jenny Sampirisi, and everyone at BookThug.

Many thanks to my mother and father, Michelle and Greg, and
my brother, Benjamin, for their support and encouragement.

Thanks to all my other families and friends in Calgary and else-
where. More thanks to everyone past and present at the University of
Calgary's English Department especially Vivienne Rundle, James El-
lis, Christian Bök, Stefania Forlini, David Bateman, Harry Vanderv-
list, Jason Wiens, Victor Ramraj, Janis Svilpis, Katherine Zelinsky,
Barb Howe, Anne Jaggard, Brigitte Clarke, Shaun Hanna, Paul Zits,
Drew McDowell, Sungfu Tsai, Mark Giles, Ryan Fitzpatrick, Chris
Ewart, and Stephanie Davis.

COLOPHON

Manufactured spring 2011 by BookThug in an edition of 500 copies.
Distributed in Canada by the Literary Press Group: www.lpg.ca
Distributed in the USA by Small Press Distribution: www.spdbooks.org
Shop on-line at www.bookthug.ca

Type+Design: www.beautifuloutlaw.com

BOOK
PRODUCTION
WAR ECONOMY
STANDARD